Finding
Grace

Praise for Daphne Greer

Finding Grace

"Recalling her own experiences at a Belgian boarding school, Nova Scotian author Daphne Greer has crafted a compelling work of historical fiction that is a poignant family drama.... The multilayered plot is intricately woven and well paced. The resolution is emotionally satisfying, making this a story that will appeal to a wide range of readers."

–Atlantic Books Today

Jacob's Landing

Silver Birch Nominee, 2016 Ontario Library Association

Hackmatack Award Nominee, 2016–2017

"Like a perfect summer day—warm, but with just a kiss of breeze—Daphne Greer's book celebrates the best things about foster care, family, friendships, and bridging the generations to make our own truths. This is a book you'll want to hug."

–Finding Wonderland

"Authentic and sensitive.... It is nice to see a protagonist whose home is a foster one, but who is not the stereotypical "troubled" youth we so often see. Greer's story will appeal to a wide variety of readers."

–Canadian Review of Materials Magazine

"A well-paced tale. Greer teases out hints about the family secret in each chapter, a tactic that should hold readers' attention as they, too, try to crack the mystery."

–Quill & Quire

Camped Out

Hackmatack Award Nominee, 2018–2019

"There's a lot packed into this slim book. Lessons about compassion and understanding, likeable characters and a story that keeps the reader turning the page to find out what happens next."

"Greer brings summer camp to life with her descriptions of campfires, canoeing accidents and elbows-on-the-table dining hall antics. Her straightforward writing will appeal to kids who enjoy realistic fiction. *Camped Out* is also an easy read that will entice some reluctant readers Kids will be able to identify with Max; like all of us, he has family struggles. But ultimately, he's just a normal kid."

–**Christine McCrea**

Maxed Out

YALSA Quick Picks nominee, 2013

"Greer tells this story with genuine empathy as Max copes with his mom and brother, protects Duncan from a local bully, and sneaks in some fun with Ian.... [*Maxed Out*] will engage reluctant readers without talking down to them or sounding stilted."

–**Booklist**

"A realistic portrayal of a family rocked by the sudden death of their husband and father.... Greer delivers a well-written, engaging novel for preteens who will be drawn in by the apparent sports focused cover and the sports related theme but who will ultimately be exposed to a book that digs a little deeper and that turns out to tell a much more important story."

–**Canadian Review of Materials Magazine**

Finding Grace

Daphne Greer

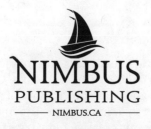

NIMBUS
PUBLISHING
— NIMBUS.CA —

Nimbus Publishing Limited
3660 Strawberry Hill Street, Halifax, NS, B3K 5A9
(902) 455-4286 nimbus.ca

Printed and bound in Canada
Cover design: Graphic Detail Inc.
Cover image of Tildonk convent school by Bernadette Barton
NB1337

This story is a work of fiction. Names, characters, incidents, and places, including organizations and institutions, either are the product of the author's imagination or are used fictitiously.

Library and Archives Canada Cataloguing in Publication

Greer, Daphne, author
Finding Grace / Daphne Greer.
Issued in print and electronic formats.
ISBN 978-1-77108-691-2 (softcover).--ISBN 978-1-77108-692-9 (HTML)
    I. Title.

PS8613.R4452F56 2018   jC813'.6   C2018-902893-9
                                                C2018-902894-7

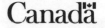  

Nimbus Publishing acknowledges the financial support for its publishing activities from the Government of Canada, the Canada Council for the Arts, and from the Province of Nova Scotia. We are pleased to work in partnership with the Province of Nova Scotia to develop and promote our creative industries for the benefit of all Nova Scotians.

For TOGS, wherever you are.

We are born in one day.
We die in one day.
We can change in one day.
Anything can happen in just one day.

AUTHOR UNKNOWN

Author's Note

WHEN I WAS FIFTEEN YEARS OLD, I ATTENDED A boarding school run by Ursuline nuns, like the one I've written about here. My dad was stationed in Brussels at the time, and he wanted me to return to Canada having learned how to speak French. When he discovered a boarding school that had a naval-like uniform, he was overjoyed. What my dear dad didn't realize was that learning French would not be my highest priority– instead, I had to learn how to navigate the nuns, who at times were quite frightening, with their strict and unusual rituals of living in a convent where "turning pre-adolescent girls into young ladies with high moral hygiene" was the main focus. Instead of French, I learned about resilience, which in the long run is far more important.

It has been widely reported that during the war Jewish children were hidden at convents in Belgium, but I couldn't find out if that had happened at the particular convent I attended. To the best of my abilities, all other references to the historical details are accurate; the personal stories, though, are fictional, as are the individual nuns and characters.

The photo of the stairs on the front cover, however, is a staircase from the convent I attended and was taken by Bernadette

Barton, a former student. She specifically took the photo because, in her words, "I wanted to catch the loneliness and sadness I felt whilst sitting on the steps and looking out the window."

At school, the students (who were mostly British) were meant to speak French at all times around the nuns. We spoke English amongst ourselves, though. I wanted to give the essence of the nuns speaking French, but have written their speech almost entirely in English—to save the embarrassment of my inability to properly speak the language. I take full credit if I have messed up the beautiful language.

Chapter 1

⁜

The Convent for Girls, Belgium
1975

"PSST, GRACE? ITH MOI."
"Yes, Dotty," I mumble from underneath my blankets. "I know it's you. What do you want?"

"My eyths won't go to thleep."

"Mmmm...just tell them to close," I say, rolling over.

"They won't."

"Mmmmm...I'm trying to sleep."

"But we didn't give each other butterfly kitheth." Her voice sounds like a whimper. I must have dozed off while reading to her. I glance over at Dotty, who's staring at the ceiling in the bed next to mine with her hands folded above the blankets and her baby doll tucked in beside her. I'm not sure who started the butterfly kisses, but with Dotty if you do something once, you have to do it every day. Sighing, I flip off my quilt and pad over to her bed. I lean in to give her butterfly kisses with my eyelashes.

"Bonne nuit," I say.

"Be back thoon," she then repeats over and over to herself. Dotty can't say the letters, no matter how hard she tries. I lie in bed listening to her whispering until her words slur and she falls asleep. Ever since I can remember, Dotty has always said "Be back soon" over and over at bedtime.

Sometimes I wonder if they were the last words our own mother said to us. There isn't a day that goes by when I don't wonder where she is. I'm starting to think she doesn't know how to find us.

I'm sure she never meant to leave us.

Here.

Forever.

I toss and turn all night. My mind zips in and out of different events like a mixed-up movie going backwards and forwards, remembering when we used to sleep together in one bed because Dotty had a bad habit of wandering at night. After a few scary nights of searching the nuns' quarters only to find her rocking back and forth near the infirmary each time, Sister Jovita started safety-pinning our nighties together so that I'd notice when she was trying to get out of bed. Sister Jovita said Dotty's late-night roaming had more to do with the fact that she was born with an extra chromosome, which fills her with more love than common sense, but I think she was just plain scared of the dark. Like me. Even though Dotty is fifteen years older than me.

As much as Dotty drives me mad sometimes, she's nicer than some of the boarding school students. They tease me endlessly about my "mongoloid sister who has the face of a chimpanzee." Dotty listens to me rant about how horrible they are, and at the end she always says, "Juth breathe, Dotty. Ith okay," which is her way of saying not to worry about it.

I wish I had more of her ability to just be her own self and not worry about what people think. In a way, I depend on Dotty just as much as she depends on me, but I guess that's what sisters do.

In the morning, when the first bell rings for morning prayer, my body feels heavy as if I haven't slept much. I rub my eyes before glancing over to see if Dotty is up, and then I remember.

She's dead.

Up until a week ago, my world revolved around Dotty. I only know that now.

Now that she's gone.

❖

Monsieur Castadot, the groundskeeper, sits in the back pew of the little chapel with his head buried in his hands, waiting for the funeral to begin. He's always been kind to Dotty and me.

Sister Jovita leads me to the front pew, where we sit next to Mother Superior, who takes up two spaces. I cover my nose at the smell of incense burning. Dotty hated the smell, said it made her "nothe want to throw up." Mother Superior leans in and tells me to sit up straight and put my hands down.

I try to listen to the service, but my mind is too busy worrying about what's going to happen to me now that she's gone—now that I don't have to help look after her. I feel like bolting out of the chapel, like Dotty used to do when she'd had enough. Before I act on impulse, Sister Jovita squeezes my hand and says, "It's time." She hands me the long matchstick and points to the altar and just like that, I move forward, whether I like it or not.

Suddenly the music floods into my heart. It pulls me into a stream of images of Dotty: her jumping-up-and-down hugs at the end of each school day, as if she hadn't seen me in months. The way her eyes danced when she'd tilt back her head to laugh. Her ability to never stay mad at anyone—no matter what they said or did. The hymn ends and I return to the ritual of the service, light the candles, and blink back tears.

After the service, I follow Sister Jovita to the graveyard. A gentle breeze blows around and amongst the trees, causing them to flutter and hum as if they're singing a comforting farewell song to Dotty. Out of the corner of my eye, I notice Sister Francis standing underneath the walnut tree. Why is she here? She never liked Dotty—or me. I move in closer to Sister Jovita and listen to the low deep voice of the priest. A pine box gets lowered into a freshly dug hole. I squeeze my eyes shut and try to push out the recurring image of her body being burned in the incinerator on the property.

⁘

Days later, droplets of rain slide down the pane and splash onto the windowsill. *"Come on, Grathie,"* I hear Dotty squeal. *"Thtick your tongue out and tathte the rain. Ith yummy."* I push the window up, take a deep breath, and try to remember her. Some moments are easier than others. As if coordinated by the convent, Dotty's death happened a week before the new school year started. Everything familiar was ending.

One last glance back at our room is all I allow myself. Two beds, a night table, and all the memories of her. I grab my suitcase and don't look back.

Goodbye, Dotty.

Chapter 2

✤

"GRACE, DEAR, PUT SOME PEP INTO YOUR STEP.
You look like you're cleaning the floor with your shoes," Sister
Jovita says.

"I'm coming," I mumble underneath my breath. I follow
Sister Jovita down the wide hall, both of us walking really close
to the wall. It's something that was instilled in Dotty and me as
a way to practice humility, but I've never understood what that
really means.

I peek into the kitchen to see who's working, but it's empty.
The stool Dotty used to use sits tucked into the corner. Because
the convent didn't have the right kind of schooling for Dotty, she
helped in the kitchen and laundry. And because she missed me
too much while I was in school, I'd have to dart back the second
classes were over—otherwise the whole convent heard her hollering. Sometimes I felt more like her mother than her sister, but
Dotty and I were stuck together, whether I liked it or not. The
nuns made sure I knew it. If I complained about it, I'd get the
lecture: "You've been blessed with a roof over your head since the
day you were born. The least you can do is help us with Dotty."
It wasn't a suggestion; it was an expectation.

I half expect her to appear, dragging the stool across the
floor so it screeches. "For the love of the Lord, Dotty. Pick up

the stool," the Sisters would say. "I forgot," she'd say every time. I think she knew what she was doing, because she'd cover her mouth, giggle, and then look at me as if to say, "Oopth."

"Grace, please stop lollygagging."

I follow the swish of Sister Jovita's long grey robe with a heavy sigh. We pass the dining hall and walk up four flights of stairs.

"Here we are," she says, sounding relieved to have made it up the stairs without needing a rest.

I have never been in this part of the convent before. We pass through a dimly lit hallway, past a small bathroom off to the right, before entering a large dorm with dark panelling and high ceilings. A small table with a brass bell on it stands guard in the middle of the room. The smell of wood and emptiness fills the air. Beige curtains held open by long tassels separate twenty *chambrettes*, each with its own bed, sink, mirror, chair, and armoire.

Sister Jovita stops in the middle of the dorm in front of an empty chambrette. "This will be yours."

I drop my bag and plunk myself down onto the mattress. It creaks when I lie down.

"You look comfortable," Sister Jovita says.

"It's a little lumpy."

"I don't think a little lump will harm you. Now, let's get you unpacked."

Sister Jovita opens my bag. My clothes have been neatly packed. Dotty and I used to do our laundry together. She always rolled her clothes. Folding was "tho hard." I miss seeing the rolls. My laundry number, 145, is sewn onto my very own uniform: a navy-blue sailor skirt and top with collars, cuffs, and my very own cravat. I've never been allowed to wear the school uniform before. Instead, I wore a *tablier*, a blue pinafore that buttoned up like a light overcoat. When I asked Sister Jovita why I wasn't allowed to wear the uniform, she explained that because I wasn't an official boarding girl, I had to wear my tablier instead. "And the uniforms are expensive to make," she added. "Everything costs money, Grace. Someday you'll understand this." Another reminder that I was to be grateful for what I had.

"Do I really have to stay here?"

"Grace, dear, we've been through this many times. Life moves forward. Things can't be the way they were. Besides, Mother Superior feels it's best that you join the other girls in the dormitory and get on with your schooling in a more dedicated way. You'll be much happier with children your own age. Keep in mind we've worked endlessly on your English, so I know the language barrier will not be a problem."

She's right about that. Once Dotty's health started slipping, Sister Jovita took it upon herself to give me private English lessons, being English herself—it made the most sense. She must have known that Mother Superior had been planning on moving me all along. I just thought she was trying to keep my mind off of worrying about Dotty. The rest of the nuns spoke only French, and the girls were forbidden to speak English except between themselves outside of class time and away from the nuns. I tried to practice with Dotty, but she made it so confusing I stopped.

"But the girls don't like me." I feel my lower lip tremble.

"Whatever would make you say such a thing?"

Images of Dotty and I being chased up the tower stairs during the girls' free time on Saturday afternoons as they shouted, "Sister retards don't belong here!" flash through my mind.

"It's just a feeling," I say.

Sister Jovita sits down next to me. "Life has a way of placing people into your life at the right time, dear. You've lived far too long without having the joy of friendships with children your age. I'm here if you need me."

She reaches into the pocket of her robe. "I have something for you. Close your eyes." She places something in my extended hands. When I open my eyes, photos of Dotty stare back at me from a little album.

"She was a dear soul, full of light and love," Sister Jovita says, pointing to a picture of Dotty when she was little. "Just like you."

Bells ring in the distance; Sister Jovita stands up. "I must dash. Hurry and put your things away and promise me you'll mind Sister Francis."

Just the mention of her name makes my stomach hurt.

Back when the girls chased Dotty and I up the tower, we found our way back and ended up in the cloisters—an area forbidden to the students. Just when we thought we were safe, Sister Francis discovered us. "What on earth are you doing here?" she hissed.

Before we had time to explain, Sister Francis demanded we hold our hands out in front of us. She took out her key ring attached to a long thin piece of leather. Dotty's hands shook as if we were in the middle of an earthquake. We had been in this position before. I closed my eyes, but when I heard a heavy thump, I opened them. Dotty was sprawled out on the floor on her stomach with her arms spread out as if she was making a snow angel. "Dotty ith bad," she repeated over and over.

Dotty and I had witnessed nuns in training doing this when they had something to confess, like shutting a door too loudly or talking when they weren't supposed to. I don't think we were meant to see it, but we did. We had lots of time to wander and explore places we probably weren't supposed to, and that's when we'd run into a new batch of nuns in training. Dotty latched onto this behaviour. She only needed to see it once for it to become a habit.

As if completely ignoring Dotty's wails, Sister Francis said, "Very well. Grace, you'll take penance for the two of you." I winced as the keys dug into my knuckles, causing them to bleed, but I held back my tears.

"Forgive us," my voice cracked. "For we have sinned."

Dotty continued sobbing on the floor.

"I pray you won't grow up to be like her," Sister Francis said, looking at Dotty. "Now, kiss my feet and promise to never visit this area again."

"We promise," I said. My lips trembled as the words tumbled out. I smelled sweaty stockings and stale incense from her robe as I knelt down to kiss her shoes.

"I expect you to practice humility by never speaking of this to anyone," she said.

Before she left, she turned and said, "Dotty! Arise in the name of God." She left before Dotty stood up with her tear-stained face.

Later that night, when Sister Jovita noticed my hands at bedtime, Dotty started saying, "Juth breathe, Dotty. Ith okay."

Sister Francis's voice echoed in my mind. "Never speak of this—to anyone."

"Um...Dotty and I were being chased...um...in...the gardens," I said. "Near the back wall...when Dotty saw a butterfly and chased it in amongst the rose bushes. She fell against the stone wall. I got scraped really badly trying to help her."

Sister Jovita hugged me. "Oh, bless your heart." Then she looked at Dotty. "You do get carried away, don't you?"

Dotty never spoke about Sister Francis, but when she'd see her in the corridors, she'd often stop dead in her tracks and pee in her underpants.

The sound of shoes clicking against the hardwood floors brings me back to the dorm. I slip off the bed and peek between my curtains to see who's coming. Maybe Sister Jovita forgot something. My stomach tightens when it's not her.

Sister Francis marches towards my chambrette. Her robes drag along the floor, making her look even shorter than she is. "*Vien ici.* Come away from those curtains. You look ridiculous clinging to them!"

My legs don't want to move, but somehow I manage to make them. She stares at me with her piercing eyes and pinched lips.

"Are you forgetting something?" she asks.

I immediately curtsey and give a little head nod as if she's the Queen of England.

"There will be no special treatments," she says, brushing past me. "You'll be treated like everyone else. You've had enough coddling as far as I'm concerned. You're not the first child to lose someone, and you won't be the last."

Her words slam into me. I bite my lip, trying to stop my emotions from sweeping across my face, but my eyes fill up with water regardless. I don't know why she's so mean. Maybe she didn't like us living with the nuns, but Dotty wouldn't have it any other way. She'd cry and cry whenever the topic came up about me moving into the dorm with the girls.

"Stop this nonsense!" Sister Francis orders. "There's no need for crying. Put your clothes away. The girls will be arriving from England shortly. And brush that unruly hair of yours, for goodness' sake."

Without another word, she leaves.

I touch my hair and think of how Dotty used to say I looked like one of the angels in the paintings in the front foyer. I feel my eyes well up when I hear her voice whisper in my head, *"Juth breathe. Ith okay. Be back thoon."*

Chapter 3

❖

IT'S EXACTLY TWELVE STEPS FROM THE CURTAIN TO my bed and six steps from the armoire on the right to the rusted sink on the left. I count the steps again just to make sure. Dotty used to pace when she was upset about something. I guess I'm a bit like her that way.

I peek out from the curtains every few minutes. No one yet. I plunk myself on the bed. The springs squeak and groan as if the mattress is upset to have someone sitting on it. I unfold the school uniform Sister Jovita left for me.

Folding it and unfolding it, I remember all the times I secretly wanted to wear one. I'd imagine playing with the other girls while wearing the uniform. I feel guilty for even thinking it now. I slip the blue sailor top over my head, step into the pleated blue skirt, pull up the brown socks, and nestle myself by the window, waiting for the girls to arrive.

When I have children, I'll never send them away to boarding school.

From the window, I have a clear view of the entrance to the convent. I keep my eyes peeled on the black iron gates. I notice two rickety army buses off in the distance heading towards the school.

A flurry of activity occurs at the front door. Several nuns holding umbrellas line the entrance to greet the girls. I press my face against the glass to watch them climb off the buses. The sound of their chatter drifts up as they run to avoid getting wet from the rain.

I take one last glance at the photo album and then tuck it underneath my pillow.

A herd of clomping shoes and chatting girls enters the dorm. Within minutes, twenty thirteen-year-old girls talking at once take over. "First one there gets dibs on their old bed from last year!" a girl yells.

I open my armoire doors and rearrange my clothing again. With my curtain closed, I feel safe and protected listening to their conversations.

"Who's nicked my spot?" someone says from the other side of the curtain. Without waiting for me to answer, a girl with long red hair whips open my curtain.

My throat is suddenly bone dry. I recognize Deirdra, one of the girls who chased Dotty and me several times.

"Grace?" she says.

I glance down at my feet.

"I thought you lived with the nuns. What are you doing in my old spot?"

"Deirdra!" An older girl with a clipboard and a whistle around her neck shouts.

"Kitty, are you really going to follow me all over this god-forsaken prison?" Deirdra pelts back. "You've been on me ever since the boat ride over!"

"Put a sock in it, Deirdra. Maybe try being nicer and see how that works for you," Kitty says. "You've just lost a point—not the best way to start the term."

"I think you're taking this 'prefect' thing a little too far," Deirdra says, stomping off.

Kitty doesn't say anything back; someone else has her attention.

"You all right, then?"

I'm relieved when I recognize Fran, a short, plump girl with huge brown eyes and brown, frizzy hair that puffs out perfectly.

"Stay away from that one," she whispers, glancing over at Deirdra. "She's beastly."

A couple of times a week, Dotty and I helped down in the cellars where the bread is baked. She was surprisingly fearless when we had to navigate the corridors underneath the convent. My mind tended to wander to something scary grabbing me, but not Dotty. Most students dreaded the task of collecting the bread, or *tartine*, so they darted out as soon as we handed it to them. Their voices echoed off the stone walls as they ran off, scared silly, but Fran—the brown girl, Dotty called her—always stayed and talked to us for a few minutes.

"Oh, and you might want to take your Sunday uniform off as well," Fran adds quietly. "We only wear it then. Your white shirt and skirt are what you need now."

My face feels hot. Of course they just wear it for church or special occasions. I feel dumb that I didn't remember that. "Thanks," I say, before ducking back into my chambrette. I close the curtains behind me, then ever-so-carefully peek through the opening and watch as Deirdra dumps her belongings in the chambrette directly across from mine. A couple of girls sit cross-legged on her bed, whispering and laughing while she unpacks.

I close my curtains, flop down on my bed, pull the pillow over my head, and try to tune out the cackle of Deirdra's laughter.

❖

At evening prayer, Mother Superior sits in the middle of the audi-torium at her desk with her back to the doors. Her grey robe flows out around her, making her look like she's growing out of the ground, or like she's a statue. A brass bell sits on the edge of her desk.

I'm still not used to evening prayer, at least not how they do it over on this side. Dotty and I were never invited here. I trip on something just as I'm about to kneel down on the row of benches that line the room, which sends me crashing into Fran.

"Oh, sorry," I whisper as I get myself up.

"It's okay. I'm pretty hard to flatten," she says, pulling her-self back up onto her knees.

One of the buttons on her shirt pops open. She smiles and fastens it back up.

"Better landing next time," a smirking Deirdra says.

"Deirdra!" Fran hisses. "You're going to get us into trouble!"

Deirdra rolls her eyes.

Without any warning, a hand clamps down on my shoulder. "*Soyez silencieux!*" Sister Francis hisses in my ear. The pressure from Sister Francis's fingers digging into my shoulders lasts long after she leaves. I squeeze my eyes shut and bow my head. The low rumble of everyone saying prayers in French together vibrates in my chest.

After the last prayer, Mother Superior rings the bell to announce, "Sustained silence has begun. There is to be no talk-ing until tomorrow after breakfast. Let the quietness of God's spirit embrace each and every one of you as you practice outer silence."

I rub my knees after standing up. It feels like we've been saying prayers for a whole year.

I'm glad Dotty and I said our own prayers, our own way. Dotty's favourite was to say, "*Thank you, thank you, thank you, for Grathie,*" followed by, "*You're welcome, God. Amen.*"

"*Petites*," Mother Superior announces, "*s'il vous plaît, venez en avant*."

The youngest students obediently start lining up, followed by our dorm, the *moyennes*, and then the seniors. In single file, we inch our way towards Mother Superior to say goodnight.

Each one curtsies in front of her before picking up a little packet of biscuits to take up to their dorm as a bedtime snack. The last petite walks by, sucking her thumb while twirling a piece of her hair.

Besides the sound of feet scuffing along the hardwood, the only words spoken are when we say "*merci*" after receiving the biscuits, followed by, "*bonne nuit*." I fall into line and follow everyone up the stairs. The echo of shoes clomping throughout the stairwell sounds like a herd of elephants. After the petites head into their dorm on the second floor, the clomping gets quieter.

Sister Francis stands at her desk in the middle of the dorm like a bulldog.

"You were a disruption at evening prayer!" she says to me as I enter. "I see that it's going to take some work to shake the Dotty out of you."

I'm not sure what she means by that, but she has the same look of disgust she used to have when Dotty misbehaved. I bow my head to hide the look of embarrassment that I know shows on my face.

I'm about to apologize, but then remember sustained silence and that I'm not allowed to talk. It would be like her to test me. Instead, I curtsey and head straight to my chambrette to change for bed. I place my clothes neatly in my armoire and join the girls in the lineup for the bathroom. Deirdra struts to the front of the line with her pink fuzzy slippers and satin pajamas. The entire time I have my fingers crossed that Sister Francis won't say anything more to me. Luckily, she's looking for something in her desk and doesn't notice me. After the last person uses the loo, we kneel down on a small piece of carpet in front of our curtains for one final prayer.

God must get tired listening to so many prayers.

"Lights out in *dix minutes*," Sister Francis announces.

In bed, I sit hugging my knees as I look out the window before flattening the lumps in my mattress. Lights twinkle from the houses in the village. I feel a wave of emptiness thinking about Dotty. I reach for the photo album. Just as I glance at the last page, the lights go out.

The dorm is pitch dark. My eyes try to adjust. I inch myself farther down in my bed so that the blankets come up around my face. One person sneezes and another coughs, then someone says, "Who puffed a dart?" followed by giggles somewhere in the dorm.

"Who's speaking?" Sister Francis barks.

Dead silence.

Sister Francis mutters something to herself. I hug my pillow tighter as if it were Dotty.

The nun's robe swishes as she moves briskly up and down the dorm. Light flickers from her torch, bouncing off the curtains and ceiling. I clench the blankets tightly as her footsteps come closer to my room. My eyes widen when my curtains billow in and out.

Please don't come in.

I hold my breath and close my eyes until I can't hold them any longer. I open one eye. My curtains are still.

Phew.

Sister Francis has moved on.

I roll over and, out of habit, flutter my eyes as if I'm giving butterfly kisses to Dotty. *"Juth breathe. Ith okay. Be back thoon."*

Chapter 4

⁂

SISTER FRANCIS'S BELL JOLTS ME OUT OF A DEAD SLEEP.
I sit up and listen to hear what the girls are doing. I'm hoping it
was the wake-up bell, but something tells me I might have slept
through that one. Ever since Dotty died, I toss and turn at night.
When morning comes, I feel like I've just gone to sleep.

I scramble out of bed and stand in the middle of my room
in a daze. I want to peek out of my curtains, but I'm too afraid
to look stupid. Instead, I sit down on my bed like a prisoner and
stare at my curtains billowing in and out as someone walks by.
That someone turns out to be Sister Francis.

She whips open my curtain and says, "You may have been
spared our morning routine, but you'll abide by it now." She
points to the little carpet that sits in front of my sink. "Place that
outside your chambrette and put your chair on top of it—then
strip your bed. *Vite!*"

I do as she says, then rip the sheets off as if my life depends
on it. Dotty's photo album falls to the floor. I snatch it up and slip
it underneath some clothing in my armoire.

Sister Francis rings her bell just as I manage to flip my mattress. Within seconds, everyone kneels in front of their chambrettes
for morning prayers. The second we're finished, Sister Francis rings
another bell, then says, "Get dressed and make your beds."

Water pipes groan from everyone brushing their teeth. The swish of curtains opening and closing replaces our voices, which must remain silent until after breakfast. This was something Dotty just couldn't do, but she did try. *"Ith tho hard to not talk, Grathie."*

When Sister Francis rings the bell yet again, I'm lying on my bed, trying to tuck in the corner of my sheets. I throw my blankets on and scramble to join the girls as they make their way down for breakfast.

At the top of the landing, Fran stands waiting. The buttons on her shirt hold on for dear life. Her skirt is yanked up a little too high, but it probably helps keep her buttons from popping. She waves. My heart sinks a little when I realize she's waving at another girl.

I glance over the railing before going down the stairs. A steady stream of white shirts and blue skirts bobs down ahead of me. On the second floor, two petites come out of their dorm holding hands and giggling.

"Shhhh—no talking," a prefect says.

The two petites zip past her and scoot down the stairs. I follow the group and line up with the rest of our dorm in front of the dining-room doors.

Mother Superior walks in among the girls, stopping by a petite who has one knee sock up and the other one crumpled down.

"Tirez vos chaussettes," she says, pointing to her socks. The little petite immediately bends down and pulls the errant sock up.

Mother Superior then walks to the front of the line and pulls out her bell from her robe pocket to ring it. The sound gets everyone's attention, then she opens the doors.

It doesn't take long for everyone to file into the dining hall. Chairs scrape until everyone is seated at the long rows of tables, thirteen to a table. The dorm nuns sit together at the back of the hall, while a prefect sits at the head of each table. I'm relieved when I realize we've been placed at assigned tables and Deirdra is not at mine—but Fran is.

"Let us pray," announces Mother Superior. *"Merci, mon Dieu,* for this day, for our food, and for the grace of God that lives in each and all of us. Amen."

The sound of pots banging and the odd noises drifting across the hall from the kitchen make me think about when I used to slip down into the kitchen when Dotty wasn't feeling well, and how I'd pull up a stool and watch the nuns prepare the meals. Glancing around, I have the feeling my visits to the kitchen have ended. The girls at the front of the table dish out breakfast. The sun dances in through the large windows, reflecting light off all the spoons as the meal is eaten in silence.

Breakfast doesn't take long with only porridge being served up. Dotty and I always ate in the kitchen; we never knew when she'd have a hollering fit. For breakfast, we ate one and a half pieces of homemade bread with a chocolate spread lathered on them.

Dotty was picky.

The porridge is lumpy.

After we finish and the bowls have been cleared by the same two girls at the front of the table, Mother Superior rings her bell. Everyone glances to face her. "As you know, we work on the honour system here," she says. "At this time, I will ask those of you who spoke this morning to please stand up."

A few people look like they're considering standing, but in the end they don't.

"Very well. If it comes to my attention that one of you has broken the rule, there will be a penance."

This prompts a few chairs to scrape as the petites who were talking earlier rise, along with two older girls.

Mother Superior jots down their names before saying, "Sustained silence is now over. You are dismissed for class."

The noise level shoots up, with more scraping of chairs and the relief of being able to speak once again.

"Oh, I thought I was going to burst. It's so hard not to yak in the morning," Fran blurts out to the girl she's walking with.

"I don't think it would take much for you to burst!" Deirdra says, laughing and linking arms with her friends as she walks past.

Fran's smile fades.

I walk a few steps behind her and listen. She sounds like she'd be nice, but I don't know how to say I'd like to get to know her better, and then I feel guilty about possibly getting a friend now that Dotty is dead.

By the time I reach the etched-glass classroom doors at the end of the hallway, the porridge is stuck in one big blob in the pit of my stomach.

Everyone is seated when I enter the classroom. There are two empty spots, one up front and one near Deirdra at the back. I take the one up front. The teacher doesn't waste any time diving right into schoolwork.

"Last year, we followed the lives of important people in history," he says. "I thought this year we'd take a different slant and explore our own history by researching our family trees."

"What if our family doesn't own any trees?" Deirdra asks.

The class laughs. If the nuns were the teachers, Deirdra wouldn't be so bold. I feel bad for him. He takes a deep breath and continues.

"I'll be passing out a sheet of paper that will help get you started. You will be required to write to your families to get all the information you need. I'm giving you plenty of time to get this project done. Each one of you will present your finished work to the class after Christmas holidays."

Everyone groans.

"Discovering and celebrating your family history can be very powerful to your own sense of self."

I stare at the piece of paper. It has a section for your mother's side of the family and a section for your father's. A lump lodges in my throat. I was left on the steps of the convent in a basket with a cloth diaper tucked in my blanket—just Dotty and me. I guess our parents couldn't handle both Dotty and a new baby. Maybe they'd had enough of taking care of people after fifteen years of Dotty. I can't stand up in front of the class with a blank page.

"My auntie is marrying one of the Bee Gees, which will make them my family," Deirdra says so everyone can hear.

On Saturday nights, Dotty and I would often sneak over to the dance hall and listen to the senior girls blare songs from their record players while they danced. We'd lie on our stomachs and peek through the banister railings so they didn't see us. *"I love the Bee Geeths,"* Dotty would whisper.

Chapter 5

⸬

THE DAY DRAGS ON WITH NO END IN SIGHT. DURING
last class, I sit by the window and watch the nuns' grey robes
floating up and down ladders in the apple orchard while I half listen to the teacher. I stretch to see if Sister Jovita is one of them.
When the bell rings at the end of the day, I lag behind the rest
of the girls when they go outside to play. It feels strange not to
have to run back to the nuns' quarters to be with Dotty. I feel
strangely out of place; everyone has a special friend already. If it
hadn't been for Dotty, I might have made a special friend by now.

Laughter carries across the courtyard from some of the
moyennes trying to keep their balance as they roller skate past
me. Their sounds fade as I get closer to the orchard behind the
rickety old tennis court. The history project thumps about in my
head as I look for Sister Jovita in the orchard. Maybe she can help
me figure out my family tree—and then, maybe, I'll find out how
to reach my mother. She would want to know that Dotty has died
and that I'm all alone. I'm sure of it. I'm sure it's a big fat mistake
that she hasn't come back.

I'm about to grab an apple to eat when I notice Sister Jovita
step down off a ladder. "I was just thinking about you," she says,
walking towards me with a basket of apples. "Isn't the smell in
the orchard glorious?"

"Yeah."

Sister Jovita lifts her left eyebrow.

"Yes, I mean." Nod, then curtsey.

Sister Jovita places the basket of apples on the colourful carpet of leaves covering the orchard floor. I crunch the leaves with my shoes. She lifts my chin and looks me in the eyes. "You look a little glum. Shall we go for a walk? Maybe then you'll be able to tell me your worries."

I follow her out of the orchard and onto one of the paths in the garden. The willow tree branches sway around us like we're in an enchanted forest, except we're only a few hundred feet from the convent. I kick the leaves along the path the entire time.

"I have a project to do in History and I can't do it!" I finally blurt out.

"Why not?"

"We have to do research on our family. I can't stand up in front of the class with just Dotty's name on my family tree. Everyone will laugh. I must have family somewhere. I mean, we had to come from *someone*."

Sister Jovita puts her arm around me. "You both were a gift to us, but as far as other family goes, I'm not—"

The sound of a squeaky wheel causes Sister Jovita to turn around midsentence.

Monsieur Castadot pushes a wheelbarrow full of shrubs. A younger man walks a few steps behind him with a shovel in his hands.

"*Bonjour*, Sister," Monsieur Castadot says. He tips his hat, then tousles my hair like he's done ever since I was little. "*Bonjour, ma petite*," he says, then glances back at the young man, who's talking to himself. "I'm trusting it's okay that Ethan comes with me today. Forgive me for not asking permission first."

"I won't say a word," Ethan says. "Just like we talked, but it's hard. Isn't it?"

Monsieur Castadot puts his arm around Ethan. "Where are your manners, my son? Say good day to Sister Jovita."

Ethan bows his upper body like he's just performed something on stage and is receiving a standing ovation. "It's a good day, Sister Jovita."

She smiles, but the look in her eyes doesn't match it.

"I had some extra shrubs lying around the shop," Monsieur Castadot says. "I figured today was a good day for some planting before the ground gets too hard. Now that Ethan has returned from being away, I have the extra help."

I look back and forth between Sister Jovita, Monsieur Castadot, and Ethan. It's like they've forgotten I'm standing here. Ethan turns his attention to crunching leaves with his work boots while they talk. I find myself smiling. Dotty used to like crunching leaves too.

"Bless you. We certainly appreciate everything you do in the gardens," Sister Jovita says, glancing back towards the convent. "I don't see any harm. That would be lovely."

"It's a good day, right?" Ethan says to me. He then bends down and grabs an armful of leaves, throws them up in the air, then laughs. This time I laugh out loud.

"Come along, Ethan. We've got work to do. We can't take any more of Sister Jovita's time."

Monsieur Castadot tips his hat. Ethan gives another big jump and crunch with his boots before following Monsieur Castadot. Then he turns and says with a big smile, "I'll be back soon."

Church bells ring off in the distance. "Oh, my—I didn't realize the time," Sister Jovita says, glancing at her pocket watch. She is suddenly all twitchy and jittery. "I'm sorry, Grace; I really must run."

"But you didn't answer my question for History."

"I'm sorry," Sister Jovita says, and then yanks up her robe to just past her ankles and darts along the path like she's in a race.

"But—you forgot your apples!" I yell after her, but she doesn't turn around.

Sighing, I decide to eat one of the apples. I start thinking about my project and how weird Sister Jovita acted when I hear someone shout my name.

"Grace?" the shout comes again.

I turn around. It's Deirdra. What could she possibly want?

"We were just about to play a game and we need another person."

"Um, I'm kind of busy, but thanks anyways."

"Don't be daft. It wasn't a question. We need another person and we've chosen you."

"What?"

"Well, it's like this. We have a tradition here that when a new girl comes they have to do a dare."

I glance at the other girls, who have gathered behind her and look kind of sheepish.

"I'm not a new girl. I've lived here all my life."

"You didn't live in the dorm, so that doesn't count."

"What do I have to do?"

"That's the spirit," Deirdra says. "See that statue over there?" She's looking a little drab these days."

"I don't get it. What am I supposed to do?"

"Tart her up," Deirdra says with a smug look on her face.

One of the girls steps forward and hands me a plastic bag full of different types of lipstick, rouge, and eyeshadow.

"You want me to put makeup on her?"

"Unless you're afraid to."

"I'm not—I just think it's really dumb."

"Dare's a dare," Deirdra says with her arms folded.

"It will be good for you to be with girls your own age." Sister Jovita's words hammer in my head as I walk towards the statue. If she only knew.

Chapter 6

✥

"YOU'VE GOT FIVE MINUTES," DEIRDRA HISSES.

I haul myself up onto the statue and cling on for dear life before inching myself around to get at her face. It isn't until I look up that I realize it's the statue Dotty and I used to sit and talk to. Dotty. She said she liked her because she was a "good lithener." She named her Miss Lovely. *"Mith Lovely."*

"Here! Take it!" Deirdra says, passing me lipstick. "Put it on nice and thick!"

I bite the lid off and spit it onto the ground. My hands shake as I smudge the fire-engine lipstick onto Miss Lovely's lips.

"Smear it on her cheeks, too!" Deirdra orders. "And then her eyes!"

"I don't think she needs any—"

"Just take the shadow!"

I bend down to reach the stupid shadow, then fumble with the case. "I need both hands to open it. I can't—"

"Oh, don't whinge—throw it to me."

I hug the statue while Deirdra gets the eyeshadow ready. Why couldn't I have said no? I start imagining that I'm hearing one of the nun's bells or keys—something. "Did you hear that?" I ask.

"There's no one around, but hurry just in case," Deirdra says.

I have to stand on my tiptoes to reach her eyes. Deirdra's whispering something to her friends, but I can't make it out.

After a few minutes, I start feeling a cramp in my foot. "I gotta stop—"

Deirdra doesn't say anything. In fact, she's strangely quiet. I glance down.

Great. They've left. I peek around the other side of the statue. One of the Sisters heads up the path. Luckily, she's not looking in my direction. I jump down, snatch the makeup bag, and shove it underneath my shirt before running off in the opposite direction. My heart pounds in my chest as I dart down the path.

"Grace?" the Sister's voice catches up to me.

I stop and turn around, hoping she doesn't notice the bulge under my shirt.

"Where are you off to in such a hurry?" she asks.

"Um...I'm just in the middle of a game of rounders."

"Oh, that's wonderful, dear. I'm glad you're making friends. Run along, then."

I dart off before she suspects something. Before I know it, I'm at the back of the garden near the graveyard. Taking deep breaths, I slow down and walk towards the stone wall and rest. Everything looks the way it should—as if nothing just happened—but I know differently.

The wrought-iron gate squeaks when I pull on the handle. My feet keep moving forward in and around toppled headstones. It's not until I notice the pile of dirt from Dotty's grave that my feet come to a standstill.

I freeze.

I'm not sure I really want to see her grave so soon. Before I know it, I'm spilling my guts as if I were at confession. "I did something really awful, Dotty. I'm going to be in so much trouble. I don't know what to do."

"The girl is back."

I whirl around. Monsieur Castadot stands a few feet away. His tweed hat and brown jacket lie across his empty wheelbarrow. Ethan smiles at me.

I stand up and brush the dirt from my hands.

"Is everything all right?" Monsieur Castadot asks. His voice is gentle and soothing.

I don't know what to tell him. The truth is, I'm terrified—what will Sister Francis do if she finds out? I blink back tears.

"She's sad. Why is she sad? It's not good to be sad—I think I'm sad now," Ethan repeats over and over as he paces back and forth.

"She'll be fine, Ethan. Carry on raking the leaves, please."

Monsieur hands me a handkerchief from his pocket. "Ma petite. Are you sure I can't help you with something?"

I shake my head. Afraid I might tell him what I did to the statue, I mumble, "I better go."

I don't say goodbye—I bolt up the hill, leaving the gate wide open. I take a different route back. I end up at the grotto, a huge rock cave that has a statue tucked in an alcove at the top. Inside the cave is a rickety wooden table. Dotty and I never knew what the cave was used for, but we both liked hiding in it. I crouch down so no one sees me. My mind jumps around like popping corn on a stove. If I go back to the statue and try to wipe the makeup off, no one will ever know. But what if someone catches me doing that?

Muffled voices off in the distance take me out of the ongoing discussion in my head. Back on my feet, I peek out from the edges of the grotto. A bunch of senior girls walk in a long row with linked arms in my direction. I quickly slip out and duck behind the grotto. I crouch down and pray that no one's seen me.

Before too long, the girls have settled themselves in the grotto and the smell of cigarette smoke fills the air. "Where are you hiding your fags?" one of the girls asks.

"In my tissue box. The nuns never look in it during inspection," another girl replies.

"Brilliant."

"So, anyone know about the makeup on the statue? I wouldn't want to be the person who takes the fall for that one."

"Oh, I'm sure some Goody Two-Shoes has already snitched by now."

"Should make for an exciting night at evening prayer."

Everyone laughs.

I feel like throwing up.

Off in the distance the supper bell rings.

"We better scram," one of the girls says.

I wait a few minutes to make sure they're out of sight before I leave. Fear has settled into my legs and they feel like rubber by the time I arrive in the dining hall as supper prayers are about to start. I squeeze in beside Fran and sit down with a heavy thump. I catch Deirdra smirking at me from the opposite table. I try to keep an eye on her during prayers.

"You all right? You look like you've seen a ghost," Fran whispers once prayers are over. She must have noticed me looking at Deirdra. "Something's up with Deirdra. Look at her," Fran says.

My jaw tightens. If Dotty hadn't died, this wouldn't have happened. Fran gets interrupted by another girl before I have time to answer her. I barely eat my meal because my stomach feels like I'm eating rocks. The conversations around me buzz in my ears and compete with the conversation I'm having in my head about how stupid I was to fall for Deirdra's prank.

After supper, Mother Superior rings her bell for announcements. "Those of you needing adjustments to your uniforms, please report to the sewing department immediately after supper."

"That would be me," Fran says, standing and re-fastening a button the moment Mother Superior finishes announcements. "Do you want to come with me?" she asks.

I'm so desperate to have someone to talk to. "I guess I could."

Fran talks nonstop about everything and anything. I'm glad she's going on and on, because it takes my mind off of the statue, but she ruins it when she says, "So why didn't you and Dotty sleep in the sister dorms? How come you stayed with the nuns?"

"A sister dorm? I didn't know they even had one. Do sisters get to sleep together?"

"Yeah. No matter how old they are. And if you're triplets, like the Mackenzie sisters. They sleep in a room above the study with three beds and a bank of windows in it. I've only been in it once, but it seemed really cozy, and no one really supervises them at night. It's just off the dorm on the third floor." Fran opens a door that leads down a long hallway. "Seems so weird you and Dotty were raised away from the boarders. Because let's face it, most of the nuns here are not the most motherly people in the world."

"Except for Sister Jovita," I say.

"Yeah, well, she's different."

"Dotty was a bit of a handful." I say. "That's probably why we didn't sleep in the sister dorm."

But the truth is, there's a lot I'll probably never know.

"So, was it weird living here with the nuns your whole life?" Fran asks.

"I guess, but I don't really know anything different," I say.

"Sister Jovita said that my mom and dad couldn't look after us—I know it sounds weird, but I secretly keep hoping that some-day they'll come back for us."

"That doesn't sound weird," Fran says. And that was all it took for Fran and I to be sealed as best friends forever.

"What happened before supper?" Fran asks, changing the subject just as we're almost at the sewing room. "You really did look like you'd seen a ghost." Her big chocolate brown eyes make me think of how Dotty used to look at me, pleading with me to "Thing a thong or read another thtory" at bedtime.

"Are you sure you won't tell?"

"I'm not daft. I can blab better than anyone, but I also know when to keep something to myself."

I end up telling her everything, just like I used to do with Dotty. It feels so good to finally have someone to talk to.

"I should have known Deirdra would try to do something like this."

"Why is she so mean?"

"I think she started her period. My mum gave me the big talk before I came this year—something about how one minute you're nice and then the next you're a bit barmy in the head."

"Sister Jovita gave me a talk about periods too, but she never mentioned I'd turn evil." I suddenly remember Dotty screaming every time she had hers. It was as if each time she forgot it was going to happen. I'd have to run to the bathroom, calm her down, and get Sister Jovita.

"Let's pray for rain tonight, so it washes off," Fran suggests.

"Too late—some of the seniors noticed it. I heard them talking at the grotto."

"They don't know who did it, do they?"

"No."

"Then pray like there's no tomorrow," Fran says, looking around. "All this prayer business has to be good for something!"

And just like that, my secret bonds us.

✦

At evening prayer, I do what Fran suggested. When Mother Superior rings her bell, it startles me, and I almost scream, but manage to catch myself.

"Before sustained silence begins," she says, "I need to discuss something of a serious matter." She pauses and then continues. "It has come to my attention that the statue of our blessed Mary has been defaced!"

My knees practically collapse. I keep my head bowed so no one will see my burning cheeks.

Mother Superior walks by every student, her keys jingling with every step. "Who is responsible? Stand up *maintenant!*"

I bite my lip.

No one moves except for a few crying petites.

"Petites, you may head up to your dorm. This clearly doesn't involve any of you." The little feet dart out of the auditorium.

Mother Superior doesn't waste any time. "Developing the right sense of direction in life is essential. And taking ownership of one's actions is imperative. Especially if one wants to become a proper young lady. I'll ask again. Who is responsible?"

I shift nervously, swallow hard. *"Juth breathe. Ith okay."*

Chapter 7

⊹

IN THE MIDDLE OF THE NIGHT, RAIN POURS OUT OF THE
sky. It sounds like rocks hitting the metal flashing on the windowsill. The rain is so heavy I can hardly see the lights of the
village as I kneel to look out. My prayers worked. The makeup
will wash off.

In the morning, the sun streams brightly into my chambrette, I have to squint. Maybe I dreamed the rain. Fran and
I stand in the bathroom lineup and she mouths the words "It
rained last night!" I want to hug her.

Out of habit, right after breakfast I head to the kitchen to
collect banana peels from the cook while Fran is at her piano
lesson. Dotty and I used to put them on the roses every Saturday
morning. "God's best fertilizer," Sister Jovita told us once, and
Dotty used to say, "The banana peelth keep the dirt warm when
it rainth out."

In the garden, I stop dead. Sister Jovita is standing on a
stool scrubbing the statue. Red streaks of lipstick stain her face,
chin, and neck. So much for the rain washing things off.

"Sister Jovita. Um…I can help you…if you'd like." I put down
the bucket of banana peels.

Sister Jovita turns around. "Oh, bless you, Grace. I'm having so much trouble getting it out of the cracks."

I shift nervously from one foot to the other. "I bet the person who did it didn't really mean to make a mess. It probably was an accident."

"I find that hard to believe."

"Do you think they'll rot in hell?" I blurt after a few moments of watching her.

"Now, why would you say such a thing?"

"Well, Dotty said she was supposed to rot in hell, but that you saved her."

Sister Jovita drops the cloth in the bucket and wipes her hands on her apron. "Dotty sometimes got things twisted up, dear. The person who did this is not going to rot in hell, but let's hope they realize what they did was shameful." She sits on a bench next to Miss Lovely.

"Can I ask you a question?" I say, standing at some distance.

"Of course, dear."

"Do you think...well...do you think I'm going to get sick like Dotty?"

"No dear, she was born with Down syndrome—you know that. Her heart was weak from the day she was born. She was never expected to live a long life. It was part of her condition."

"My heart hurth," Dotty said a lot in the last year of her life. I feel bad now. I hadn't really taken her that seriously. I thought she was just complaining because she didn't want to do what I wanted. Dotty could be pretty dramatic.

Sister Jovita pats the bench. "Come sit." She puts her arm around me and says gently, "I know you miss her. We all do."

We sit in silence for a few minutes.

"Grace, dear, what else is troubling you?"

I bite my lip and look away. "It's just that—"

I swallow hard. It's now or never. "I put the makeup on the statue."

"Oh, godfathers."

⁘

In Mother Superior's office, there are paintings of old people wearing long robes and crosses around their necks, and it smells musty. I sit alone. At the sound of her voice coming up the hallway, my stomach does a little flip.

"I'll ring for you when I'm ready," Mother Superior says to someone.

I immediately stand up, nod, and curtsey when she walks into the room.

"I hear you've been busy," she says, shutting the door.

My face flushes. The smell of incense follows her as she bristles past me. The keys she wears on the belt of her robe clink with each step.

"Grace, when I suggested you go live in the dorm with the rest of the girls, I thought it would be good for you. I didn't expect we'd be having this conversation. What on earth would possess you to commit such a disgraceful act, to the Virgin Mary no less?"

I stare at the floor. I can't look at her.

"Grace!" she barks, making me jerk. "You have explaining to do."

"Um...I...I...."

She stares at me. The wrinkles on her face make her look like an old toad.

Outside her window, girls are playing a skipping game. I wish I were with them. "It was a dare," I finally whisper.

"For goodness' sake, don't mumble, and sit up straight like a young lady."

"It was a dare," I repeat a little louder.

"I see," she says, opening up her top drawer and pulling out a pad of paper. "I need names, then."

Scrunching up my skirt, I try to think quickly. If I tell her it was Deirdra, who knows what Deirdra will do to me?

"I see this isn't going to be easy," she says, taking a deep breath. "I trust Fran isn't part of this, or she'll be seeing the bricks of Brixton Row before the week's out."

My head starts to whirl. I can't let her think Fran had anything to do with it. She's been so nice to me.

Mother Superior reaches into her pocket and pulls out her watch. "I don't have all day. Who put you up to this?"

Deirdra's name is on the tip of my tongue, but for some reason what comes out surprises not only Mother Superior but me as well. "Me."

"Pardon moi?"

"It was me."

Crossing her arms and leaning back into her chair, Mother Superior sighs. *"Mon Dieu,* give me strength," she mutters under her breath.

"I, um..." I ramble quickly, not really thinking about what I'm saying. "I guess...um...I thought she'd look prettier with some makeup on. So I dared myself to do it." I feel my face turn a thousand shades of red. "Some of the seniors left their makeup lying around, so...."

Mother Superior stares through me. Her lips are pinched as she breathes heavily through her nose, like she's ready to explode. Then her expression eases and she says, "We all make choices in life, Grace. Some have God's blessings and some don't. It's up to you to learn to trust yourself, and to know what is right and wrong—clearly an area you need to work on."

She pushes herself up from the desk. "Very well, then; I'll speak to Sister Francis about finding some things to keep you occupied, since you're obviously having trouble entertaining yourself in an appropriate manner. You shall pray tonight for forgiveness." She stands up. "Let this be a warning, Grace. There will be no second chances."

I'm not sure she believed my story, but I'm relieved when she doesn't press me any further.

Chapter 8

⁜

SISTER FRANCIS SITS AT HER DESK READING A NEWS-
paper with white gloves on. I stop dead in my tracks when I
notice a black strap lying across her desk. She doesn't move, just
continues to read the paper as if I'm not in the room.

My eyes dart around. The dorm is empty. I feel like bolting
out of there just like Dotty would do.

"So," she finally says, lowering the newspaper, "I gather you
weren't able to occupy yourself without getting into trouble."

I curtsey and keep my head bowed as I speak. "I'm sorry,
Sister Francis, I really didn't mean to. I was—"

"Keep your excuses to yourself!" she snaps. "You're just
like Dotty," she says, pulling off her white gloves with their ink-
stained fingertips. "But I guess that stands to reason, doesn't it?"

She places the white gloves neatly on the table next to the
newspaper. "What you did was a disgrace to the church and an
embarrassment to us all."

I clench the sides of my skirt and brace myself as she picks
up the strap and moves away from her desk. "If it were up to me,
you'd be living elsewhere, but I don't have a say."

Why does she hate me so much?

"Step forward and give me your hands."

They shake as I hold them out.

"Turn them face up."

The first smack feels like a swarm of bees stinging my hand. The second smack is like my hand is on fire. After that I lose count. I close my eyes and look away. I bite my lip and try to will my tears to stay inside, but it's no good. They stream down my cheeks until I can taste the saltiness in my mouth.

Sister Francis finally stops.

"Go to the kitchen and get some cleaning supplies. The statue is to be perfectly clean when I take my walk in the garden in an hour. Am I clear?"

I nod.

"I didn't hear you."

"Oui, Sister Francis." My voice quivers as I curtsey and then slowly back away. Once out of the dorm, I glance at my hands. Big red welts cover my palms. I can barely move my fingers.

I hate her.

❈

"Blimey, Grace. Why didn't you rat out Deirdra?" Fran says when she finds me outside.

"I was afraid of what she'd do to me."

"Well, she wouldn't have given you the strap, I can tell you that! Wait until I see her!"

"Forget about Deirdra. I've got to get this done. Will you help me? I've tried, but it stings too badly."

"Of course I will."

Fran grabs the cloth from the bucket and climbs onto the base of the statue. "It looks like someone's already given her a once-over."

"Well, if it's not Tweedledum and Tweedledumber," Deirdra says, walking up the path with two of her friends.

"Deirdra! You're just plain beastly! Look at Grace's hands. She got the strap because of you!"

Deirdra flinches. For a second her eyes show some feeling, but she erases any amount of heart when she opens her mouth. "Well, only a retard would get caught. I guess that's not a stretch, considering who your sister was."

Before I can say anything, Fran dumps the soapy bucket of water over Deirdra's head.

"I can't believe you did that!" Deirdra sputters as she wipes her face. "You're such an idiot."

"Oh, poor you! You're lucky Grace didn't rat you out. Now get out of here!"

"I hate you both!" Deirdra screams before storming off.

"Forget about what she said," Fran says, jumping down from the statue. "She's gone barmy. Come on, let's get some fresh water."

I try to grab the bucket but drop it immediately when the welts on my palms touch the handle.

"Here," Fran says, picking up the bucket. "You wait here. I'll go fill it."

"Thanks." My hands sting with anger at Deirdra, Sister Francis, and myself. I plunk down on the nearest bench and stare at the red welts. What fills a person with so much hate?

The sound of squeaky wheels makes me glance up. Monsieur Castadot pushes the wheelbarrow full of leaves. "Hello, ma petite, I trust you're feeling better than the last time I saw you?"

I shift nervously on the bench. "Uh, sort of."

Out of the corner of my eye, I notice Fran coming back up the path with the bucket of water sloshing all over the place. Without thinking, I place the palms of my hands on the bench to push off as I leap up. "Ouch!" I flinch and then glance at my hands, which are now starting to bleed.

"What's happened to your hands?" Monsieur Castadot gasps.

"I...uh...."

"Oh, mon Dieu," he whispers, then gingerly holds my hands to get a better look.

"What happened?"

"I'll tell you what's happened," Fran butts in. "Sister Francis gave her the strap!"

"Why on earth would she do that?"

"Exactly!" Fran says.

"Well, I did kind of put makeup on one of the statues," I mumble.

"Because you were put up to it!" Fran says.

"Well, this is nonsense. We need to get your hands cleaned up and bandaged."

"No, no!" I say. "I can't make a scene. I'll get in more trouble. Please, leave me alone. I'll be fine. Fran, you probably have bandages in the stuff your mum sends you, don't you?" I glare at Fran and nod my head slightly.

"Crikey, I've got all kinds of bits and bobs—everything but the kitchen sink in my care package," Fran jokes. "I'll doctor her up—promise."

"I'm so sorry to hear this has happened to you. There must be something I can do!"

"I'll be fine. I promise. Come on, Fran—we better finish cleaning."

"Geez, if looks could kill," Fran says once he's out of earshot. "Just the mention of Sister Francis sent a bolt of lightning across his face. It almost looked like he was going to cry."

"I know. I guess she has that effect on everyone. You do have bandages, right?"

"Every size—my mum is a big planner. Hey, after this I've got to do some research on the convent for my History project. Do you want to come to the library with me?"

"Sure. You're lucky you can go look up stuff for your project. I don't know how I'm going to do my family tree."

"Did you ask Sister Jovita for help?"

"Yeah, but she acted really weird—said she had to think about it."

"Maybe she feels bad because she doesn't have an answer for you and doesn't want to hurt your feelings."

"Yeah, maybe."

"Or maybe you could work on the same project that I have. We have to research the history of the convent. It sounds dead boring to me. Besides it looking like a prison, I can't imagine one interesting thing I'll possibly be able to write about."

"Yeah, except I'm hoping that if I can trace my family tree, I'll find my family."

"Oh, blimey, Grace. How daft of me. Well, maybe I can help you. If you help me with my project, I'll help you with yours." Fran sticks out her pinky finger and wraps it around mine. "I won't forget about yours once mine is done. Promise."

I don't know how Fran can possibly help me, but I don't care. I latch onto her finger and repeat, "Pinky swear."

Chapter 9

✥

"PSST," FRAN SAYS, POKING HER HEAD THROUGH THE opening of my curtains a few days later. She drapes the curtains so the rest of her body looks invisible. I hear Dotty's voice. *"Look, Grathe, the brown girl's face is in the curtain."*

"Are you ready for inspection?" Fran whispers.

"Sort of, except I can't find part of my uniform; that stupid piece of white fabric that we pin in to complete the sailor look."

"It's actually to hide your cleavage," Fran whispers, trying not to laugh.

I glance down at my flat chest and make a face.

Fran darts back to her room, but instead of coming back with a spare piece of white fabric, she has a tissue. "The way she's been acting lately, she probably won't even notice," she whispers.

Sister Francis has been mixing up students' names and then yelling at them when they correct her. Yesterday she got mad at Deirdra for listening to her radio when it was free time, and we all had to sit in silence for the rest of the day.

Sister Francis rings her bell to begin inspection. We all stand perfectly still in front of our chambrettes. She inspects each room and student. One by one we hold out our hands palms down. She inspects our nails to make sure have not been biting them. She has a pair of nail clippers in her hand to snip off any nails that are too long. There's no tenderness as she clips them straight across. Fran winces.

My hands shake as I hold them out while Sister Francis approaches me. I feel the tissue slipping down to one side. I try to adjust it, but I only make it worse. She scrunches up her lips as she inspects my uniform, starting with my shoes and then all the way up to my top, where her steely eyes can't help but notice the tissue slipping down. She reaches in and snatches it out. "*Qu'est-ce que c'est*? Where is your *plasteron*?"

I stutter as I try to explain. "I...I...I'm sorry, I couldn't find it—"

Deirdra stifles a laugh from across the dorm. Sister Francis whirls around. Deirdra stands perfectly still, any evidence of a smirk evaporated.

"Pitiful," Sister Francis mutters underneath her breath as she takes out her little black notebook and scribbles something down before bustling past me to inspect my armoire.

Thankfully, I'd made sure everything was neatly folded. I breathe a sigh of relief when she moves on.

Cupboard doors creak and her clippers snap as she makes her way around the dorm, completing inspection. After what feels like forever, she rings her bell to signal it's time to line up for church. In silence, I follow the stream of blue sailor outfits and white gloves floating down the four flights of stairs and along the long corridors until we reach the massive wooded doors to the cathedral. Single file, we march into the church as the massive pipe organ booms a hymn.

The smell of incense hits me when we enter. I hear Dotty's voice in my head saying, *"My nothe is going to throw up."* Out of habit, I touch my nose with my glove, but when I catch one of the Sisters glaring at me, I immediately put my hand down. Eventually, the pews fill and the three-hour service in Latin begins.

This is when I miss Dotty the most. If I had known that this was what I was missing, I would have never have complained about always having to be with her. My time with her was way better than trying to stay awake while the priest talks for hours in a language I don't understand.

During the last hymn, I glance towards the upper top balcony and notice Sister Francis kneeling with her head buried in her hands. Why isn't she singing? I keep my eyes peeled without looking too obvious. Normally she hovers over the balcony, keeping an eye on us to make sure we're not doing things like writing notes back in forth in our hymn books. I wish Fran were near me so I could show her, but she's three rows ahead of me. Just before the hymn ends, Sister Francis wipes her eyes, kisses the cross that hangs around her neck, and stands up. I immediately look away.

After the service, we walk from the cathedral in silence to the auditorium, where we have night prayers. As if sitting on the church's hard, wooden pews for three hours weren't enough, we now have to sit through proclamation at the auditorium, where Mother Superior awards us our merits for the month. Forming two crocodile lines in order from the shortest to the tallest, we enter, and with precise timing we stand in front of Mother Superior as each class is called forward. We then sit on the pews with our knees clamped together and our backs as straight as a board. God forbid anyone cross their legs.

Those who have been good receive a gold card; anyone who has been bad receives a second degree or third degree and will not be allowed to join in the Sunday afternoon activities. Because of the makeup situation, I know my penance is not going to be easy. No surprise when I'm awarded the third degree. Deirdra, on the other hand, receives a gold card. Why didn't I say something? My penance starts immediately: while everyone else heads off to Sunday lunch followed by free activities, which sometimes includes a movie on the projector, followed by supper and disco dancing to record players, I have to go to the study hall. You'd think getting the strap from Sister Francis was enough penance.

Anger bubbles up inside me: If Dotty hadn't died, none of this would be happening. If I had told Mother Superior that Deirdra put me up to the makeup thing, none of this would be happening. I sit writing, *I have acted improperly by defacing the Virgin Mary. I am truly sorry. Please forgive me,* over and over. I become more determined than ever to research my family tree—and then, just maybe, I'll find my family, and things will get better.

⊕

A few days later, Fran and I root through books in the library, flipping from one book to another, trying to find information on the convent. The sooner I help Fran with her project, the sooner she'll help me with mine.

"Geez, it's not as easy as I thought it would be," Fran sighs. "Why do people have to blab on about things that aren't important? Can't writers just say this happened and then that happened without writing a bunch of gobbledygook?"

"Hey, this might be something," I say.

"What is it?"

"Here, I'll read it to you. 'During World War One, the convent in the little village of Tildonk, with its stone wall surrounding its massive structure, was deemed to be the perfect holding cell for the Belgians taken prisoner by the invading German army.'"

"Let me see," Fran says, leaning over my shoulder.

"Many of the pupils," I read, "were evacuated from the convent prior to the German invasion."

"No wonder this place creeps me out. I bet there's solider ghosts walking the halls at night."

We flip through more books until we find some pictures. "Hey, look!" Fran says, pointing to a black-and-white photograph titled, 'The Miracle Statue.' "You know, the one mounted on the wall with all the chipped paint pieces missing on the wall around her!" Fran continues reading from the book: "During a shooting spree by the Germans, the statue remained bullet—free. It has been regarded by many as a miracle."

"Wow! I had no idea," Grace says. "Dotty used to tell Sister Jovita they needed to fix the broken paint on that wall. Never once did she tell us they were from bullet holes!"

"She probably didn't want to freak her out."

"Hey, you could use this for the front of the project," I say, pointing to an aerial photograph of the convent.

"Yeah, sure," Fran mumbles as she grabs her pad of paper. "Ta. Just mark the page."

I stare at the photo. It's the first time I've really looked at a picture of the entire convent. It looks like a mini-kingdom, with the stone wall surrounding the buildings, the high turrets with windows in every nook, huge willow trees and orchards, frog pond, statues scattered throughout the grounds, the massive cathedral, smokestacks by the courtyard, and the little stone houses in the village that circles the wall.

While Fran writes stuff down, I continue looking for more information. I reach for another volume, and something falls from the other side of the shelf. I walk around to see what it is. I find a small leather-bound book. When I flip it open, I notice the pages at the beginning are water-stained and stuck together. I carefully try to pry them apart, but they're too brittle, so I flip to pages that I can easily read. The handwriting is small and fancy.

The Nazis entered the convent this morning. They searched the students' trunks and clothing. Guards have been placed on watch outside the convent. I'm terrified!

Mother Superior says there is no room for fear, only faith,
but it's been almost two weeks now and the fighting has not
stopped. I hope Hugo is safe.

"Is this about the war?" I mutter. It sounds like a diary. But whose could it be? I flip to another page, trying to find something with a date. Just to be sure. Most of the pages are too stained to read, but I manage to find undamaged ones a few pages later.

September 7, 1942
Dear diary,

Last night Mother Superior prepared us for our next call of duty. We are expecting Jewish children in the middle of the night who are hiding from the Germans. We are their only hope of staying alive. For weeks now the Germans have been knocking on every door in the village looking for Jews. They are treating them like animals, taking them in cattle cars to concentration camps. Their heads have been shaved so that everyone knows who they are. The English radio says they are being gassed to death once they reach the camps.

If there is a God, I don't understand how this can be happening. I hate the Nazis. Last night I had a nightmare that the Nazis stormed into the convent to take me away. Even Mother Superior couldn't convince them I wasn't Jewish. I woke to my sheets drenched in sweat. I had to rinse my face off with water. It's the one time I was grateful that the water in our chambrette jug is ice cold. I can't help but feel guilty that I'm safe here in the convent and that I'm not Jewish—I know it's wrong of me to feel this way, especially when the only reason I'm here is because father brought me and left me here. I pray every day that once I've given my time allotted here for my sins that the war will be over and Hugo will come for me. No matter what father says. Mother Superior says to me daily there is no room for fear, only faith. I turn 16 next week and I am finding it hard to not let fear take over.

I dash around the stack of books, clutching the diary. "Fran! You've got to see this!"

"What?"

"I found a diary. I think the girl lived in the convent during the war. Listen to this."

Fran sits quietly while I read the entries, before saying, "Crickey! Imagine what they would have done to me?"

"I don't even want to think about it," I say. "Can you believe the girl writing this is only fifteen—three years older than us?"

Fran shakes her head. "No, I can't, but this is brilliant. I'd say my history project has just hit the gold star."

Chapter 10

✦

SOME THINGS GET A BIT EASIER AS I GET USED TO LIFE without Dotty. Like our first morning prayer. If I don't want to get out of bed for it, all I do is turn my slippers upside down and slip them underneath my curtain, just enough to look like I'm kneeling inside my cubicle. Then I can hop back into bed. Fran taught me that.

But other things aren't getting easier—like coping with Sister Francis. When Fran hid underneath the stage to avoid going to church and Sister Francis found her, she made Fran sweep the leaves on the garden paths until her palms were raw. And when Deirdra was caught toasting a tartine on the radiator, she had to clean all the radiators with a toothbrush. Not to mention what happened when Fran was caught rolling up her skirt to make it shorter: Sister Francis made her stand in front of the dorm in her underpants for an entire hour!

I often thought Dotty's reactions to some things had been dramatic, but Sister Francis's are downright cruel.

Sister Jovita once said to me, "Sometimes the insides of a person are like a puzzle. Some have all their puzzle pieces and some don't." I'm starting to think that the insides of Sister Francis have some pieces missing, just like Dotty's did. Except with Dotty, it didn't make her mean. Just lopsided.

Heads pop up from books at the sound of the door creaking open during evening studies. Sister Jovita enters with her arms stuffed with parcels and letters. A flutter of whispers breaks out in the room.

A few minutes later, the prefect rings her bell and says, "Fifteen minutes left of study time. A reminder that letter writing to your families is due. You can come get your mail once you've passed in your letters."

A collective groan rumbles through the room. I glance at the girls reaching for their notepads. If Dotty hadn't died, I wouldn't be reminded weekly that everyone but me has a family to write to. As if I'm preparing to run a marathon, my heart tightens and I feel a sudden urge to bolt out of the room—just like Dotty would. Then I hear her. *"Juth breathe. Ith okay."*

Sadness rushes over me like a darkening sky as I try to remember her, but sometimes remembering only makes things worse, so I try to push it away. I reach into my desk to busy myself while they write their letters, which is when I notice the diary we found in the library. Fran says I can read ahead as long as I tell her about anything that would be good for the project. I figure it's the only way to get her project done quickly. I feel a little bit guilty that it's because I want her to help me with mine, but I push that away and flip around, opening to pages that look interesting.

September 8, 1942
Dear diary,

The Jewish girls arrived shortly after midnight. There were six girls in total; the youngest is seven years old. She was wearing four pairs of underpants, a dress, and over that a skirt and a jacket, with the Star of David sewn onto each piece of clothing.

A flurry of activity makes me glance up from the diary. Fran beams as she carries a huge package back to her desk. Deirdra has a letter in her hand and waves it around like a lunatic. Sister Francis is two aisles away from me. Before she gets any closer, I slip the diary back into my bag in case she wants to see what I'm reading. With one glance she'll know I'm not doing my homework.

At bedtime, something comes flying over the wall of my chambrette and lands at the foot of my bed. It's a chocolate bar with a note attached: *There's more grub in my parcel from home. We'll have a good pig-out tomorrow.*

Smiling, I slip off my bed to root around in my bag for a pencil. The diary catches my eye, so I grab it. I scribble, *You're the best,* on the back of a piece of paper, fold it into an airplane, and sail it over to Fran. A few seconds later Fran coughs, which means she got it. I crawl back under the covers, open up the diary to where I'd left off, and let the sweet taste of chocolate melt in my mouth as I read before lights out. My eyes are drawn to the next entry:

October 9, 1942
Dear diary,

I'm sorry I haven't written in a while. I've been so tied up with helping the new children settle in. Mother Superior pulled me out of the kitchen to help in the dormitories. In a way, it helps take my mind off things. The latest news from the outside is that if you're caught hiding a Jew, you are executed—in plain daylight! And if they can't find the hiders, the Gestapo grabs hostages, innocent people, then lines them up against a wall and shoots them. The papers are full of announcements refer-ring to their deaths as a "fatal accident." And here we are, hiding them in the convent. I'm terrified we'll be found out.

If only Hugo was here to protect me, especially when we have the air raids in the middle of the night. Each time, we take the children to the cellars and stay there until things are all clear. I hate the sound of planes flying overhead. In the cellars, you can hear the rumble of gunfire. We sing songs to take their minds off the horror.

I've had no news from Mother and Father, but this doesn't surprise me. I turned 16 today. No one remembered and I didn't remind them. I'm filled with dread about the future. I wish I'd hear from Hugo. If I knew he was safe, I'd at least rest a little easier.

Sister Francis turns the lights out as I finish reading the entry. I clutch the diary to my chest as my eyes get used to the darkness. I feel so badly for the girl. I'm sure we'd be good friends if I'd known her back then. I wonder who Hugo is? The lights from Sister Francis's torch flicker up and down as she does her nightly rounds. It makes me think of the Nazis on patrol. I slide the diary underneath my pillow next to my photo album and pull the blankets up around me. I curl up into a tight ball, hug my pillow, and try to hear Dotty's voice telling me to just breathe, it's okay—but I can't hear her voice. I panic and remember how she'd pretend to sprinkle magic dust on me when I was upset so I'd feel better, and how she'd pretend to blow me kisses and always end up spitting all over me by accident.

I end up reaching for the photo album. I have to squint to make her out in the dark, but when my eyes adjust, I see her chubby little hands and her smile stare back at me. I end up whispering to myself over and over, "Juth breathe. Ith okay," and "Be back thoon," until my words slur and I fall asleep.

In the early hours of the morning, I wake suddenly from a nightmare: German soldiers came into the convent and dragged me away and no one stopped them. Once I'm fully awake and know that I'm safe, my breathing slows down. The early morning light sneaks into my chambrette, making me feel even safer. Because I can't go back to sleep, I decide to read some more of the diary. I turn to a legible page.

December 16, 1943
Dear diary,

It's been a full year and I'm still consumed with deep sadness. Hugo doesn't even know. Why hasn't he written? He promised he would. I used to pray for the war to be over, but now—I have nothing to live for. He's not coming back. My baby is not coming back. My family has shunned me. I have nowhere to go. Mother Superior convinced me that it was best to take my vows. With the ongoing war, I felt that I had no choice, so I agreed.

The workload continues to be unbearable. We're on our feet from sun-up to sundown. All our supplies are so heavily rationed that we're running out of the most basic items. Laundry detergent is in short supply. We've all been sleeping on the same bedsheets for over three months. I feel so dirty. Today was the first time I'd been in the village for quite some time. It's unrecognizable with the red-and-black Nazi flags hanging off every storefront. Mother Superior asked me to visit the nice baker in the village to barter for some flour with one of the pigs we raised. He has connections to an underground source.

While I was talking to the baker, two Nazi soldiers barged in and demanded to see his identification. They kept shouting that they knew who he was. I didn't know what to do. The baker insisted that he wasn't a Jew. I had no idea if he was one or not. The Nazis wouldn't listen.

They dragged him out of his shop while his wife and I watched in horror. They kicked and punched him until he was on the ground and curled up into a ball like a child. I felt so helpless standing there. Inside I was screaming for them to stop, but Mother Superior has taught us to never cause a disruption with the Nazis, or our lives could be in danger as well, so I did nothing. I can still hear his wife sobbing as she collapsed in a heap on the doorstep of their shop. I cried too.

Then the most horrible thing happened. One Nazi got annoyed that I was crying while consoling the wife. He told me not to waste my energy on such filth. He ordered me to my feet. I was terrified. I didn't know what he was going to do, so I backed up into the doorway. He rubbed up against me and brushed his hand over my cheek, wiping my tears away. He said I was a pretty Fräulein and what was I doing being a nun. I didn't know what to say. His fingers lingered before tracing them down over my lips. He whispered into my ear that it was a pity I was a nun. His breath smelled like the bottom of a toilet mixed with cigarette smoke. I panicked and urinated right then and there. When he noticed the puddle at my feet, he screamed at me, saying I was as pathetic as the Jew baker. He left in disgust, but not before snatching a piece of cake from the display case. Once the Nazi left, I ran back as fast as I could to the convent. Mother Superior was disappointed that I didn't return with the flour. I told her what the Nazi did to the baker but not what he said to me.

By the time I'm finished reading, my jaw is clenched and my heart rate has quickened. Why were the Nazis so hateful? The poor girl was only sixteen years old. I would have been so scared. She was so brave. I close the diary and wedge myself next to the window and peer out. The village is starting to wake up, with a few cars on the road and the odd person going for an early morning walk with their dog. It seems so peaceful compared to what I've just read.

When Sister Francis rings the first bell in the morning, I'm more than wide awake. I can't wait to tell Fran about the diary.

Chapter 11

❖

"I'M GOING TO PARIS FOR HALF-TERM, I'M GOING TO Paris..." Deirdra can't stop bragging.

Fran and I follow a few steps behind her on the way from class. We're so busy rolling our eyes at Deirdra that we don't notice when she and her friends stop suddenly. Fran bumps smack into her, knocking her forward.

"Are you daft?" Deirdra shouts. "I suppose you're trying to hear about my fabulous plans at half-term?"

"Oh yes." Fran puts her hands together like she's about to pray. "Do tell. Where is Daddy taking you?"

"Well, since you've asked, we're going to Paris for three nights, and then we're going to the south of France to stay in one of Daddy's villas. If we have time, we're going to—"

"Come on, Fran. Let's go," I whisper.

"We'd love to stay," Fran replies, linking arms with me. "But thanks to you, Grace has to report in with Sister Francis after class for the rest of this term, to let her know what she's doing to keep herself occupied."

"Oh," Deirdra says, glancing back and forth between Fran and me. "Just a second," she says to her friends. "You didn't say anything about the makeup, did you, Grace? I mean, it was just a joke, right?"

"What, afraid Daddy might change his plans if he found out what you did?" Fran says.

"Belt up, Fran. Did you say anything, Grace?"

I take a step back. "No, I didn't."

"Well, that's good," Deirdra says loudly, then turns back to her friends and walks away with them as if we've suddenly disappeared into thin air.

"You could have strung her along for a little bit," Fran says.

"You know, for a minute, I thought she was going to say sorry or something."

"The old Deirdra might have," Fran says. "You know, back in England, when we were little, we lived on the same street. We were pretty good friends. And then her mom and dad divorced and her dad remarried this lady with funny hair and really long nails. Deirdra started getting mean, so Mum made me stop chumming around with her."

"Is her stepmum really *that* bad?"

"Well, let's just say she's a bit stuck up and doesn't care for Deirdra one little bit. Last year at half-term, Deirdra was supposed to stay here, but instead she got invited home with a friend who lives near her own home. When she surprised her dad, her stepmum was furious, and made her dad send her back on the train to the convent the next morning—said something about having a dinner party and it was inconvenient."

"Wow."

"Yeah, and, get this—her stepmum wears those padded knickers to make her bum look all full and everything." Fran prances around sticking out her bum before darting up the stairs to the dorm. Our laughter echoes off the walls and chases us up the steps. It fades away when we reach the narrow hallway that leads into the dorm.

Fran and I stop talking once we enter. Nothing irks Sister Francis more than listening to "mindless chatter," as she puts it.

It appears no one is in the dorm. Sister Francis's table sits empty, and everyone's chambrette curtains are neatly pulled back and tied with their tassels. Fran stops in the middle of the dorm to listen: a leaky tap, a creaky radiator, and nothing else. "I'd say we've got the digs to ourselves—for a bit, anyways. I'll wait with you until Sister Francis arrives," Fran says, heading towards my chambrette.

"Don't you think it's weird she's not here?" I say, opening up my armoire doors.

"Maybe she forgot. Remember, she couldn't think of my name the other day, and she went through a string of names until she just called me missy?"

"Yeah, she's been doing that a lot lately," I say, placing my school bag on the bottom shelf. I notice the diary sticking out. I pick it up and face Fran. "Wait until I tell you what I read last night. You won't believe it."

Fran flicks off her shoes and gets comfortable on my bed. "I'm all ears."

I sit down next to her and open the diary, turning to where I left off last night. I get goosebumps as I tell Fran about the German soldiers beating up the Jewish baker and what one of them said he did to the girl. "So, did you start reading from the beginning of the diary?" Fran asks.

"No, I couldn't. The pages are all stuck together and they're super delicate. I was afraid that they'd rip. I just flip around and read random pages, but I'm kinda hooked where I am."

Fran shrugs. "Okay, just read where you are, then."

I get comfortable on my bed, turn to the page I had saved, and start reading.

I continue to do what Mother Superior says, I pray, I serve, I place others' needs before my own, and yet none of this stops the war or helps me get past what has happened to me.

*To make matters worse, only forty minutes away in Mortsel,
allied bombers dropped twenty-four tonnes of bombs over the
wrong area. In eight minutes, 936 people were killed and 1600
were injured. We only know the details because of the underground newspaper Mother Superior gets, but I remember viv-
idly the roar of the planes flying over us.*

*I keep thinking about it all happening in only eight min-
utes. That's how long it takes me to walk from my chambrette
all the way down to the cellars to collect bread. It could have
been us. Still no word from Mother and Father or Hugo.*

"Did you hear something?" asks Fran.

I stop and put down the diary. "Go check," I whisper.

Fran slips off the bed and peeks out through the opening in
the curtain. "I don't see anyone." She zips back to the bed and
flops next to me. "This diary is practically writing my history
project. Keep going."

I'm about to start reading again when Fran grabs my arm
and urgently puts her fingers to her lips. We hear the clicking of
shoes and then they stop. After a few minutes of silence, we carefully slip off the bed and stick our heads through my curtains.
Sister Francis is on her knees with her back to us, praying by her
bedside. I think she forgot I was supposed to meet her. I make
a face, which sets off giggles in Fran. She plugs her nose to stop
herself from laughing out loud, but a burst of giggles manages to
slip out. Before I know it, we're both in stitches.

"Who's there?" Sister Francis asks.

I grab Fran's arm and point to the diary. She scrambles to
get it and shoves it underneath my pillow seconds before Sister
Francis whips open the curtain.

Chapter 12

❖

"WHAT ARE YOU DOING IN HERE?" SISTER FRANCIS demands. Her habit tilts to the side and bits of her grey hair dangle against her face.

I look at Fran, curtsey, and then mumble, "Um…Mother Superior said I was to come see you after school to let you know what I was doing—so that you'd know I was occupied in a proper way, because of what I did—and I was asked to see if you needed help…."

"Why would I need any help?" she shoots back. "I was just…." She glances back towards her own room, then clutches her cross and puts it to her forehead and mumbles, "Archangel Michael, please help me—"

Fran's eyes go wide. I'm so glad she is with me to see her acting so weird.

Sister Francis stares blankly. An uncomfortable silence fills the space. She looks like she's searching in her brain for something to say.

"I might have the wrong time," I say.

"Um, maybe we should leave," Fran adds. "You know—go breathe in some of God's clean air in the garden."

"*Mais oui*!" Sister Francis snaps. "*Vous*! I remember!" She shakes her fingers at me. Her little body brushes past Fran, forcing her to move out of the way. Fran falls backwards and lands partly in my armoire, making the hangers clang together. I don't have time to laugh at the sight of her wedged in amongst my clothes, because Sister Francis grabs my left earlobe and twists it.

"Owww!" I yelp.

"The garden is the last place you're going," she hisses before letting go. Her eyes dart about my room. "Now, what is this?" she says, noticing the small photo album peeking out from my pillow. When Fran jammed the diary underneath the pillow, the photo album must have pushed out the other side. She picks it up and opens it.

"It's of Dotty." My voice trembles. "When she was little...."

Sister Francis looks at it closely for what seems like a lifetime. It's almost like she's forgotten we're all crammed into my chambrette together. She whispers, "If only I could have—" And then, as if a bolt of lightning has hit her, she slams it shut. "There's no need for you to have such reminders. You'll only become a whimpering little child."

"But Sister Jovita gave them to me! They're mine!"

"I'll look after this from now on."

"That's not fair!" Fran butts in.

"Excuse me?! This does not concern you, young lady."

"But—"

"One more word from you and I'll be washing that mouth of yours out with soap."

"I hate you," Fran says underneath her breath.

"That's it!" Sister Francis says, grabbing her by the arm and dragging her into the middle of the dorm. She whips her head back towards me. "*Viens ici*, Grace! Bring your chair. And collect Fran's at the same time." Her words are curt, and she holds Fran by the scruff of her neck as if Fran is going to bolt out of the dorm any minute. "Place them right here." She points to the middle of the dorm.

I place the chairs side by side. Sister Francis lets go of Fran and snatches the chairs, then positions them back to back so that we're both facing in opposite directions.

"You're to pray for forgiveness. It's clear you both need cleansing, inside and out! Kneel on the chairs and count your blessings."

What blessings?

I kneel on the chair and stare into my room. If I were a little bit to the right I could see out my window and imagine myself somewhere else, but instead I'm stuck staring at my sink and the head of my bed, where my photo album should be safely tucked underneath my pillow.

I bow my head, close my eyes, and pray I'll get my photo album back. It doesn't take long before my back aches and the cane holes in the chair pinch the skin on my knees. I adjust my skirt to protect them, but it's too short. So I pray for time to speed up. Fran sighs every now and then.

Sister Francis rummages around in her cubicle the entire time.

"I think she's going barmy," Fran whispers.

Sister Francis is strangely quiet for the longest time. I hold my breath and pray she didn't hear Fran. I blow out air when I hear the creak of Sister Francis's armoire door closing. Maybe that's where she's put my photo album.

Once the hour is up, she rings her bell and says, "Let this be a lesson, young ladies. I'll not tolerate rudeness from either one of you." She adjusts her habit and straightens out her robe. "Put your chairs away and then go down to the cellars to collect the tartine for tonight's supper. Afterwards, head to the petites' dorm and help with bathtime."

Sister Francis glares at us. I don't dare rub my knees. I don't want to give her the satisfaction.

"Would you look at my knees?" Fran blurts once we're out of earshot. Red welts in the pattern of the cane chair cover her kneecaps. I glance down at mine—same thing. I touch them gently. They are sore and tender to touch. Tears well up in my eyes.

"Are you okay?" Fran asks. "The welts will go away, give them a few seconds to bounce back."

"It's not my knees. She's nicked my photo album! You saw the look in her eyes—she's not giving it back."

"Oh, don't be daft! We're getting it back. Trust me on this one."

For some reason, I believe her.

We link arms to walk through the long corridors leading into the tunnels that take us to the cellars. The smells of old earth and stone fade away and the scent of fresh bread gets stronger the closer we get. The comforting smell eases the fear of getting lost in the endless tunnels. We keep to the middle, trying to avoid the cockroaches that hang out in the cracks of the stone walls. Every now and then we step on one. The crunch makes me scream.

"I'll never get used to that sound," Fran says, darting forward after stepping on one.

"Me neither!" I say, grabbing her sleeve.

Just before we reach the cook ovens, Fran points to a tunnel on the left that disappears into the darkness. "I wonder if that's where the girl in the diary hid during the air raids."

"The *diary!* It's still underneath my pillow!"

"Well, I'd say you've got a horseshoe up your *derrière,*" Fran says, laughing. "If Sister Francis knew we nicked it from the library, she'd likely have ripped your ear right off!" She takes a step towards the darkened tunnel.

"What are you doing?"

"Just getting a feel for what it must have been like to hide in here." Her voice echoes off the walls and repeats itself farther down. Fran takes a few more steps. She's not very far in, but I can barely see her.

"Fran, maybe you shouldn't go too far...."

A crunching sound underfoot sends Fran darting back out of the tunnel.

"Yup! That's enough research for me. It's kind of scary in there. Let's get out of here."

Fran and I link arms and carry on, navigating the cold and uneven slabbed floors, until the smell of bread is mouthwateringly strong. Sister Leona lights up when she sees me. "Oh, Grace, darling. How lovely to see you."

"How's Marigold doing?" I ask.

"I think she's missing you and Dotty. She hardly sings now."

While we wait for the trays of freshly made bread, Fran and I walk over to the canary pecking at the bells hanging in her cage. "You're tho pretty," Dotty used to say to Marigold. They'd seem to chat back and forth as if they understood each other.

Sister Leona offers us both an end slice of bread while we wait.

"Geez," Fran whispers. "Sister Francis could take a few lessons from her, couldn't she?"

Marigold starts chirping as we're leaving. We drop the bread off in the dining hall for supper, then go to the petites' dorm.

"Phew," Fran says, plugging her nose as we enter. "The sweet smell of missing home. Count your lucky stars you lived with Dotty," she whispers. "You could have easily been put in here with all the bedwetters and stinky mattresses!"

I glance around the petites' dorm. Metal beds in neat rows. Little girls with sad faces. I realize I'm not the only one missing someone.

Chapter 13

✥

I NOTICE A LITTLE GIRL SITTING ON HER BED TRYING to brush her hair. "I'm going to help her," I say to Fran. "Be right back."

The mattress creaks when I sit down next to her. "Do you want some help?"

She nods and hands me her brush. I try brushing gently, but it's totally matted with tangles. "Ouch!" she yelps with each stroke. I stop for a moment to glance over to where Fran helps braid another. I signal to her to come help me when she's done. The lingering smell of pee makes me want to get the job done as quickly as possible. When I ask the girl what her name is and her little voice squeaks out, "Emma and I'm five," a lump lodges in my throat and the smell of pee seems to vanish.

"I'm sorry, Emma," I say, giving her a hug. "I'll try to go more gently."

A few minutes later, Fran plunks down on the bed next to ours and looks at the mess of tangles I'm trying to sort out. "Oh crikey, you've got yourself a little bird's nest by the looks of things."

"We're working it out, aren't we?" I say, leaning in closer to Emma. "Don't mind Fran, she's a bit goofy sometimes."

Emma giggles.

Fran tackles one of Emma's tangles. After the better part of thirty minutes, her hair is smooth.

"I think you're fine now, Miss Emma," I say, putting the brush down.

Emma gives both Fran and me a hug before darting off.

"Okay," Fran says, standing up and stretching. "let's scram before we have another rat's nest to go through."

"We should check with the Sisters before we leave. We can't afford to get into any more trouble."

"Yeah, maybe you're right."

I poke my head into the doorway of the loo and notice one of the Sisters by the sink.

"Is it okay if we leave now?"

"Yes dear, that would be fine."

Fran and I bolt out of the dorm before she changes her mind.

"I stink!" Fran says. "Phew! I smell like pee. It's in my hair and everything."

"Oh, gross, we do stink!" I say, getting a whiff of myself.

"Do you hear that?" Fran says. Music drifts up the stairwell from the dance hall. "Oh, great! It's ballroom dancing. Remember, Madame Fairbairn was making up a class from last week? We'll get docked points if we don't show."

"But we stink!"

"Maybe once we're in our gym clothes we'll smell better."

Fran and I dart down the stairs and run through the hallway until we come to the bank of windows in the breezeway that separates the front of the convent from the back.

We peer over the banister to the dance hall. The late afternoon sun floods through the stained-glass ceiling, creating spotlights on the girls dancing. The class is in full swing.

We run down the back steps, slip into the changing rooms, and grab our gym outfits from our cubbies.

"How do I look?" Fran asks, twirling around in her gym clothes: a one-piece blue jumpsuit that gathers at the waist and comes down to the knees, then puffs out like a balloon. Fran fills her outfit with no room to spare.

"Just about as good as I do," I say, twirling around. "Come on, let's go."

Madame Fairbairn has her usual layers of makeup and smelly perfume. It's a wonder the nuns don't make her wash it all off. She stops the music when she notices us arrive.

"Girls, you're late!"

"We were helping the Sisters with the petites' bath-time," Fran says, making it sound like we were doing a good deed instead of being on the receiving end of Sister Francis's discipline.

"Very well," Madame Fairbairn says, then taps her stick on the floor. "Girls, I want everyone to switch partners."

Fran rolls her eyes and sighs. "So much for keeping our lovely smell to ourselves."

Madame Fairbairn walks by each girl and taps them on the head, *"Un, deux, trois,"* until she has given everyone a number. "Now go find your matching number and line up for the foxtrot," she says.

I wander in amongst everyone, trying to find the other number four.

"Oh, let me guess...You have number four?"

I turn around to see Deirdra standing with her hand on her hip, her gym outfit fitting her perfectly.

"Lucky us," I mumble.

"Girls, step it up, we don't have much time left."

Reluctantly, I place my right hand on Deirdra's shoulder and hold her left hand. Deirdra barely touches my waist with her right hand. We both avoid looking at each other. The music starts and Madame Fairbairn yells, "Dance, ladies, dance with all your heart! I want to see you floating off the floor. Just like this." She proceeds to dance around the room.

"Blimey—you stink!" Deirdra blurts out halfway around the room.

I feel my face grow red immediately. "It's your fault."

"How is it my fault you reek?"

"Is there a problem?" Madame Fairbairn interrupts.

"No, Madame," we both answer.

"*Bien*! Now, for this dance, your faces are supposed to be cheek to cheek," she says, placing us into position. Deirdra tries to hold her breath while I pray for the song to be over. At the end of it, we both part ways without speaking to each other.

Before leaving the dance hall, something makes me glance up towards the upper walkway. I almost gasp when I notice Sister Francis peering over the banister, staring right at me with the photo album in her hands.

I whip my head away and pray she didn't see me looking at her. "Is she still there?"

"Who?" Fran asks.

"Sister Francis!" I whisper. "Look up at the walkway, but don't *really* look."

"Oh, she's there, all right! Start walking," Fran whispers. "Pretend we don't see her."

"She gives me the creeps," I say.

Fran glances back when we reach the changing room doors. "Grace!" She squeezes my arm. "She's leaving. Let's follow her."

"Are you sure we—"

"Yes, I'm sure...." Fran yanks me backwards and drags me up the stairs. Sister Francis turns the corner just as we enter the walkway. Her robe billows out as she walks quickly, heading straight for the set of French doors with flowers etched into the glass.

The doors click shut behind her.

We press our faces against the glass, hoping to see if she still has my album.

"I can't see anything," I whisper.

"Me neither."

"Okay. This is what we're going to do," Fran says.

Chapter 14

⁜

AT EVENING STUDIES, EVERYONE BUT ME HAS THEIR heads buried in their books. I sit stewing about Fran's plan.

Somehow, I have to come up with an excuse for being in the nuns' quarters in case someone catches us. Fran is going to figure out how to get the keys from Sister Francis. Then, when the nuns go on their Saturday trip into town, Fran and I are going to use her set of keys to get into my files.

The trouble is, ever since Dotty died, I haven't been allowed back into the nuns' quarters. I can't help but feel a little panicked about getting caught. I can't get the strap again. To take my mind off things, I decide to read more of the diary. Fran has officially made me the note taker, because she hates reading.

July 3, 1944
Dear diary,

Mother Superior reminds us all to offer up our sins in confession. Daily I'm reminded of mine, but I find it difficult to tell the priest anything, especially when he is breathing heavily as he listens to me. It frightens me when I can't see his face because I don't know what he's thinking. I'd rather sort out my worries within myself. I'm not like the other Sisters, who seem relieved after confession. Maybe I'm not meant to be a nun. I'm so glad I can write my thoughts in my diary. I've been hiding it in different places for fear of Mother Superior finding it. Even though I feel she has taken pity on me, I know she would not approve of my thoughts or free expression. Today I found the perfect place, where no one can find it.

I glance up from the diary and look about. Everyone is busy doing their homework. If anyone were to wonder what I was doing, they'd think I was reading from the book I've placed the diary in the middle of. I quietly, carefully turns the pages until I find another entry. I feel a little funny reading about such private things, but can't help myself.

September 7, 1944
Dear diary,

I can't speak of what I'm about to write to anyone for fear of what might happen to me, but I can't stop thinking about it. About a month ago, Mother Superior instructed me to take food to the German soldiers who were out on patrol outside our gates. I didn't want to do it, but had no choice, as Mother Superior was busy and no one else was available. It was a warm night. I remember being struck by the number of stars in the sky and the frogs in the pond were especially loud as I walked towards the front gate. My plan was to hand the food to them and return immediately inside, but then a Nazi pulled me through the gate and insisted I sit with him while he ate. I told him that I wasn't allowed. He laughed and then shoved the food in his mouth as if he hadn't eaten in days. I remember looking back toward the convent, but only the light hanging over the top of the doorway stared back and in that moment everything happened so quickly. He covered my mouth so I couldn't scream. He dragged me back through the gates into the garden, where we couldn't be seen. I tried to get away from him, but he was too strong. He threw me to the ground, knocking the wind out of me. I struggled against him, but this only fuelled his rage. I stopped fighting back, lay motionless, and prayed for it to be over. In my head I screamed, but I uttered no sound aloud. Only the high-pitched singing from the frogs in the pond filled the air.

When it was over, I scrambled to my feet and ran as fast as I could to the front steps of the convent and bolted the door shut behind me. Evening prayer was in progress, so no one was near. I ran to the front window to make sure he'd left. But he was standing smoking a cigarette and staring right up at me. I was terrified. Thankfully, a commotion occurred outside the gates that made him leave. When I knew for sure that the soldiers were distracted, I ran back outside and locked the front gates. I couldn't chance him returning. When I was safely back inside, I slumped to the floor and sobbed.

The prefect rings the bell for mail time, jarring me back to the study hall. My mind races. I don't understand how to feel after reading this. Why would the solider hurt her? How could someone be so horrible? I try to gather my thoughts, but they're consumed with more questions about the diary entry.

I reread the passage. The noise of chairs scraping and hushed whispers as students get called up to the podium for mail float around in the background. I don't feel any better after rereading it. In fact, I'm filled with more questions. I need to tell Fran.

I glance around, searching for her dark mop of hair that bounces when she walks, but she's up getting mail. Deirdra's skipping up to the podium. "It's got to be about my trip," she gloats to one of her friends. I watch as she opens her mail.

Her smile unexpectedly turns to a frown. She stares at the letter for a long time and then proceeds to fold it up. Is she crying?

Our study period ends when the prefect rings her bell. I put the diary out of my head for a while, until evening prayer, when my thoughts are consumed again by the girl in the diary.

After lights out, I toss and turn, listening to the nighttime sounds: a creaky radiator, someone mumbling in their sleep, another snoring. All are slowly becoming normal to me. But tonight, someone is crying and trying to do it quietly.

I sit up in bed to figure out who she is, but it's too hard. I slip out of bed, open my curtain, and listen. It sounds like a girl crying on the other side, but before I can figure it out, Sister Francis turns her torchlight on. I quickly slip back into bed, praying the mattress won't moan and groan like it normally does. Thankfully, the squeaks are gentle.

I listen again for the crying, but it has stopped. I roll over to reach for my photo album and remember Sister Francis has it. A quiet determination comes over me as I remember Fran's plan and hear Dotty saying, *"Juth breathe. Ith okay."*

The next morning, I wake up with an itchy head, really itchy. I scratch to the point where it hurts and remember my plan with Fran. Sister Francis rings her bell for morning prayer. I throw the covers off. The floor is cold to touch. I pad over and open the curtains, then glance over at Deirdra. She looks like she hasn't slept at all.

Fran and I exchange glances as we kneel down in front of our curtains. I'm nervous but don't want to show it. I know what I have to do. After all, Fran is doing the hard part. If she gets caught, she'll be in even bigger trouble than me.

Fran winks at me before joining the lineup to the bathroom. I close my curtain instead of going with her, then open my armoire and stare at my clothes, trying to decide what to wear after morning classes. The best thing about Saturday afternoon is that we get to wear regular clothes. I decide on my favourite pink top and oldest pair of bell-bottomed cords. Before getting dressed in my school clothes, I brush my hair really hard. The itch is not going away.

After braiding my unruly blond hair, I tiptoe to my curtains and peek out. Sister Francis is at her desk, looking in her drawer. I wonder how long it will take for her to notice my sheets are not out. I listen to chairs being placed outside of their chambrettes for the sheets to be dumped on. Every second seems to take forever. Curtains swish and cupboard doors slam shut as the girls carry on with their morning routine. My stomach starts to grumble at the thought of having more of Fran's grub from her care package.

Sister Francis finally whips open my curtains, startling me. "Just what to do you think you're doing?" she barks. "You haven't stripped your sheets!"

"Oh," I say, looking at my bed, trying to sound like I've really forgotten.

"Well, just don't stand there! Strip your sheets!"

I don't move. I know Fran needs more time to get the keys without being noticed.

"*Maintenant*!" Sister Francis orders.

Not knowing quite what to do, I blurt out, "I want my photo album back!" The second it rolls off my tongue, I want to take it back like a frog catching a fly.

"Don't be so foolish. I don't know what you're talking about," Sister Francis says, sounding impatient.

"But you took it!"

"Grace! You insolent child. I knew you'd be nothing but trouble in my dorm. Now, stop this nonsense and strip your bed!" She marches away before I can say another word. I'm stunned. Why is she lying?

Chapter 15

❖

FRAN SLIPS INTO MY CUBICLE AND HOLDS UP A SET OF keys.

"I can't believe you got them," I whisper, pulling her farther in.

Fran grins from ear to ear. I know she's dying to tell me every detail, but I don't give her the chance.

"Something really weird just happened—I asked Sister Francis for my photo album."

"You did what?" Fran gasps.

"Shhh!" I cover her mouth. "I know, I know...but listen. She lied. She said she didn't know what I was talking about. Can you believe that?"

"This is getting weirder by the minute," Fran whispers. Glancing at my bed, she says, "You better get your sheets on your chair before she comes back."

"Okay, you go before she finds you in here!" I say, pushing her out of my chambrette.

❖

"My head is so itchy!" Fran complains. We sit on the window ledge waiting for the nuns to leave for town. "And there's still three more days until we're allowed to wash our hair."

"Mine is too!" I say, scratching my head again.

"I don't know what's taking them so long to leave. Usually they're gone by now." Fran glances at her watch.

"Oh! I almost forgot!" I say. "I brought the diary. I didn't want to risk anyone snooping in my room. You won't believe the stuff I read last night." I give Fran the rundown.

"Blimey!" Fran says. "This is getting kind of deep. Let's see what else she says." Fran gets comfortable on the window ledge.

I start reading the next entry with Fran, who's keeping her eyes trained on the gates of the convent.

September 30, 1944
Dear diary,

I have not been feeling well. I don't have any energy. I've thrown up several times. It's just like before. All I want to do is sleep, but I can't. I feel like I'm losing my will to carry on. And with all the depressing news we hear from the underground newspaper, there's not much point.

The latest report says that 25,000 Jews from Belgium have now been sent to Auschwitz and that close to 24,000 have already been killed. It's hard to imagine that this is actually happening. I have lost the joy I once had. My thoughts seem to stay dark no matter what I do to keep them pushed deep down. I feel so alone.

"Crikey!" Fran says. "That poor girl."

"I know," I whisper. "But I wonder what she means by 'just like before'?"

"I don't know. I find her diary kinda confusing, but it's probably because you're only reading me bits and pieces. Oh! There go the nun-mobiles," Fran squeals, as if what we've just read has evaporated into thin air. She points towards several white vans sailing through the gates.

I tuck the diary into my back pocket and follow her down the steps. "I wonder what they do in town?" I ask.

"Who knows? Nun stuff, I guess. Come on, leg it!"

We fly down two flights of stairs, past the kitchen, and up the back stairwell that only the nuns are supposed to use.

The hallways are empty and the office doors are closed. "Let's try Mother Superior's office first," Fran says.

"I can't believe we're doing this." I glance up and down the corridor. "If we get caught—"

"Ta-da!" Fran says, opening the door.

"Okay, hurry up," I squeal, practically knocking Fran out of the way before shutting the door behind us. We both giggle, but mine's more nervous than Fran's. "I'm going to open the window so we'll hear if the nuns pull back in."

"And I'll lock the door," Fran says.

The sound of laughter and screams drift up from the playground. "I don't know how the petites don't get dizzy from going around and around on the carousel."

"Yeah, I'd barf," Fran says, already rifling through the filing cabinet. "Well, this is too easy. Here's your file!" Fran waves it in the air.

"Let me see."

Fran passes it to me and together we go through it. "Birth certificate, health records," Fran announces over my shoulder as if I'm blind. "And a note about putting makeup on the statue. Boy, they don't miss a thing, do they?"

"The photo album is definitely not in here."

"Hey, wait a minute. What's this?" Fran pulls out a stack of bank drafts from cheques written to the convent.

I grab them from her. Each one is in the amount of 150 Belgian francs made out in my name. "Who would have sent these?"

"Beats me," Fran says. "There's no name, only this address: 1359 Rue du Vaartdijk, Tildonk. Maybe it's money from the government or something, because you don't have any family. Grab a pen and write it down in case we need it later on."

"Now what?" My voice sounds deflated after scribbling the address on a piece of paper.

Fran scratches her head. "I'm thinking." She pauses. "Hey, what was Dotty's full name?"

"Dorothy Adora Dimanche."

"Sister Francis might have put it in *her* file," Fran suggests.

"That's a good idea!" I take a deep breath and flip through the files until I see her name. It's pretty thick, so I place it on Mother Superior's desk. When I open the file, her death certificate stares back at me. "Maybe you should go through it...."

"Okay." Fran's voice is soft.

I slump in the chair and hug my stomach.

Fran whips through, paper after paper, before saying, "I don't see your photo album. I'm sorry, Grace. You okay?"

I nod, unable to speak.

"I bet you it's in Sister Francis's chambrette. Let's go look. We've got loads of time."

"Shh!" I say. "Someone's in the hallway!"

"Get in the closet!" Fran hisses, pushing me towards it.

We jam ourselves in as quickly as possible. My heart thumps as I try to balance on a box in between Mother Superior's robes. The lingering smell of incense tickles my nose. I feel a sneeze building. I plug my nose until the sensation goes away.

"We have several things to discuss," Mother Superior says. "Do you fancy a glass of sherry while we chat?"

"I'd love one."

Fran and I glance at each other.

"My first concern is over Sister Francis," Mother Superior says. I almost gasp out loud.

"I've witnessed her being overly harsh with the girls, and this is the third time this month she's lost her set of keys. I've tried talking with her, but I can't seem to reach her. She's so distant and removed. I'm rather concerned. I may have to call Dr. Graham to pay a visit."

"Oh, I'm so glad you mentioned this," Sister Jovita's soft voice says. "I must say, I've had grave reservations about placing Grace in her care. She's never been very nurturing. Grace has been through so much, and while she hasn't said anything about Sister Francis, I feel something is not quite right."

"I'm concerned too," Mother Superior says. "Grace has already given in to peer pressure, which is unlike her. More urgent matters are before us, though. We need to deal with the recent outbreak of lice and bedbugs in the petites' dorm without causing a frenzy among the girls."

Fran gasps.

"Did you hear something?" Mother Superior asks.

I freeze.

"Well, now that you mention it, the petites are awfully loud outside."

"Look at that. I don't remember leaving the window open," Mother Superior says.

I hold my breath as she walks over to the window. The sound of the window slamming shut makes me jolt. I bump into the hangers, causing a faint clinking sound.

Mother Superior and Sister Jovita are quiet. I place my hands over my mouth.

"As I was saying..." Mother Superior continues.

I carefully breathe out a silent sigh of relief.

"Haircuts will be in order to lessen the burden, and then we'll treat them. We'll have to keep them quarantined until it's under control. I'll leave that with you to handle."

"In that case, I'll finish my sherry."

Chapter 16

✣

"OH, CRIKEY! WE HAVE LICE!" FRAN SAYS, UNTANGLING herself from Mother Superior's robes. "I feel soooo gross!"

"Me too! Now I really *can't* stop scratching my head!"

"I know—come on, let's get out of here," Fran says, heading towards the door. She peeks out, then signals to me that it's clear. We bolt down the hall and don't stop until we set foot on the stairs leading to our dorm.

"That was a close call," I say, catching my breath. I plunk down next to Fran, who's already collapsed on the stairs. "I can't believe we just did that. Can you imagine if they knew we were in the closet? That was way too close! Are they really going to cut our hair off?"

"Not if I can help it. I've seen what they do. A bowl gets plopped on your head and then they chop off your hair. Once you look like a complete doorknob, they put some stinky stuff in your hair to kill the bugs!"

My eyes go wide at the thought of bugs crawling around in my hair.

"Hey, I just thought of something," Fran says. "I remember my mother helping a neighbour whose kids got lice. Now, let me think...what did they put in their hair? I remember mum was so proud of herself for helping them out. She was acting all doctor-like." Standing up, Fran says, "Vaseline! That's what it was! All we have to do is rub it all over our hair and leave it on long enough for the lice to be smothered."

"What?!"

"I know it's horrid, but that's what we've got to do—then we wash our hair, and *voila*...no haircut."

"Where will we get some?"

"Mum packs me everything imaginable. Let's put the keys back, you look in Sister Francis's room, and I'll try to find some Vaseline."

"Hey, what about the stuff they were saying about Sister Francis?" I ask, heading up the stairs.

"I'm not sure what they were on about."

"I sort of feel badly for taking her keys—especially because they blamed it on her."

"I don't," Fran says once we reach our floor. "It's not like she's overflowing with kindness!"

Fran does have a point, so why do I feel bad?

As luck would have it, the dorm is empty.

"Be super quick, Fran. I don't want to be in Sister Francis's room by myself!"

"I'll be with you in a tick. Just make sure you look under her bed and everything."

My heart does a little flip-flop when I enter her chambrette. I try not to glance at the wooden crucifix of Jesus above her bed. I don't need anything more to make me feel guilty. I take a quick peek underneath her bed. Nothing. I lift up her pillow. Gross—a used tissue. "I'm not finding anything!" I mutter.

I stare at Sister Francis's armoire. Taking a deep breath, I open it. Everything is a mess, which is odd because it should be neat. I carefully lift up her clothing.

Nothing.

One of Sister Francis's habits sits on the top shelf. Something makes me want to pick it up. I stand on tiptoe and try to reach it, but can't. I put my foot on the first shelf and haul myself up and grab it.

Underneath the habit is a stack of pictures held together by elastic bands.

"Any luck?" Fran asks, joining me.

I jump down, clutching the pictures in my hand.

"Look at Sister Francis!" I squeal. We both stare at a younger picture of her, fully decked out in her nun's outfit on roller skates, and then another one of her riding a bike in the garden. "She looks half human," Fran says.

"It's a wonder her robe didn't get caught in the spokes of the wheels," I say.

"See if there's more," Fran says.

"What are you doing in Sister Francis's room?"

I don't need to glance up to know who it is. I'd recognize Deirdra's voice a mile away.

"Um...we found Sister Francis's keys and, uh...we were just putting them away," I say nervously.

"What's in your hands, then?"

"You're such a nosy parker, Deirdra!" Fran says, closing the armoire doors.

"Really?" Deirdra leans against the doorframe. "I'm sure Sister Francis will be interested to hear about the two of you going through her stuff."

"She nicked something of mine and we were looking for it!" I blurt out, still holding the pictures.

"Whoa," Deirdra says with her hands in the air. "Pardon me...a little emotional, are we?"

"Deirdra...you don't know anything about anything!" I yell. Tears sting my eyes.

"Well, I can't wait to tell Sister Francis—"

Fran doesn't let her finish. "Did you hear that lice is going around?"

"What?!" Deirdra screeches.

"Yup! Bedbugs, too. No one can go home until it's all cleared up. They're even talking about cutting everyone's hair."

"You've got to be kidding me!" Deirdra touches her hair.

"Dead serious—started in the petites' dorm."

"Oh good. It's not in ours."

"Well, um..." Fran says, scratching her head and glancing towards me.

"I think we got it when we were helping the petites," I say.

Deirdra starts backing away. "You were my dance partner! Oh, great!" She frantically shakes her perfectly curled hair. "Do I have any? Can you see anything?"

Rolling her eyes at me, Fran says, "Deirdra...listen for a minute."

"Don't just stand there! Look in my hair!" she shrieks.

"Deirdra!" Fran yells. "Stop getting your knickers in a knot." Fran grabs her by the sleeve. "We've got a plan. Can you hear me?"

Deirdra flicks back her hair.

"What?"

"Promise you won't say anything about us being in Sister Francis's room?"

"I'll think about it."

"This is serious, Deirdra. Do you want a bowl hair cut? Or better still, do you want Grace to rat on you about the makeup? Mother Superior knows someone put her up to it."

"All right! I won't say anything, but this plan of yours better be good," she says, scratching her head.

"Oh, it's good, all right. It's from a master, so to speak," Fran says. "Follow me."

I slip into my chambrette with Sister Francis's pictures. I know I should put them back, but I don't. There's something about them that makes me want to look at them a bit longer. Instead I slip them inside my pillowcase and then join Fran and Deirdra.

"Vaseline?" Deirdra says in a dry voice. "How is that going to help?"

"It smothers the lice."

"Urgg," Deirdra says, covering her ears.

"We'll still have to pick out the eggs, but at least—"

"Okay, okay, stop talking about it. I feel like I'm going to be sick." Deirdra turns towards the sink and starts gagging. "Just spare me the details," she mutters before splashing water on her face.

"All right, then," Fran says, rolling up her sleeves. "Let's slop it on, ladies."

Chapter 17

✦

"CAN WE GET THIS GOOP OUT OF OUR HAIR NOW?"
Deirdra asks.

I look at the clock. Has it really been an hour? I can't believe we've lasted this long listening to her complain.

"Yeah, we should be all right," Fran says, checking her hair in the mirror.

"I want to go first," Deirdra says, stepping towards the sink.

"Go ahead," I say—anything to get rid of her.

Fran dumps a whack of shampoo onto Deirdra's hair. After a few minutes of scrubbing, she turns the water on to rinse.

"That's freezing!" Deirdra screeches.

"It's kind of hard to make it warm, Miss Deirdra, when we only have cold water in the dorm!" Fran sounds frustrated, then puzzled when she says, "Well, this is weird."

"What?!" Deirdra asks.

"It's not coming out!"

"Blimey, Fran! Can't you get anything right?" Deirdra complains.

Vaseline sticks to the back of my neck. I pick at it with my fingers, then wipe it on my pants before joining Fran over by the sink.

"Okay, okay, just let me try it again. It has to come out." Fran squeezes more shampoo all over her hair.

"Fran, this better come out!" Deirdra shrieks. "I leave for my trip in a couple of days."

Fran rolls her eyes at me.

Can't Deirdra see that Fran is trying her hardest to get it out? "Maybe it needs stronger shampoo," I suggest.

"I have some really expensive stuff in my closet. Someone go get it," Deirdra orders. "It's in my blue bag."

"Will you?" Fran asks me.

"Sure."

Everything is folded neatly in her armoire. A picture of her dad rests on the middle shelf with a smiling younger picture of Deirdra. Her dad looks serious in his suit and tie. Deirdra's eyes sparkle as she looks up at him.

The blue bag is on the bottom shelf. It's loaded with makeup. I rummage through it until I find the shampoo. Just as I'm about to put things back, I notice a crumpled-up telegram. It's from Deirdra's dad. I glance over towards Fran's chambrette. I can't help myself. I quickly read it.

Deirdra,
I won't be able to take you on our trip. Something has come up.
Beatrice and I will be heading to Sweden. Daddy.

"Grace, did you find it?" yells Fran.

"Yup, be right there." I shove the telegram back where I found it. For a split second, I feel sort of badly for Deirdra. He didn't even say sorry or sign it with love. The trip is all she's been talking about.

"I'm sure this will help." I hand Fran the shampoo.

"Took you long enough," Deirdra gripes.

Biting my tongue, I plunk down on Fran's bed.

Fran washes Deirdra's hair three more times. "I don't know, Deirdra. It still feels really greasy to me."

"Let me see." Deirdra stands up and towel dries her hair. When she takes the towel off, I know we're in deep trouble. Her hair is so badly knotted from all the scrubbing that it looks like a bird's nest is growing out of the top of her head.

"Fran, look what you've done! I need a brush. Quick, someone get me a brush!"

"I don't think we should use them, in case they have...you know...lice?" Fran says.

"Look at my hair! What am I going to do?" Deirdra shrieks.

"What about using your fingers?" I suggest.

"My fingers? Are you seeing the same hair I'm seeing?" Deirdra plunks down next to me and puts her head in her hands. "I can't believe this is happening to me. I won't be able to go on my trip looking like this!"

Why is she pretending she's still going?

"It's your fault!" she screams at me. "I'm so daft for listening to the two of you!"

"What's going on in there?"

We all freeze.

Sister Jovita opens the curtains. "Good heavens. What on earth are you girls doing?" she says, looking perplexed.

Deirdra sucks in her sobs and wipes her tears. I look at Fran and plead with my eyes for her to come up with something.

"Girls?"

"They ruined my hair!" Deirdra wails.

"We did not!" Fran shoots back.

"Someone tell me what's going on!"

"Um...well, Deirdra here was complaining about her hair being so dry, and I heard once that Vaseline softens it. She wouldn't believe us unless we all did it..."

My eyes widen. How does she come up with these things?

"I see," Sister Jovita says. "I gather it won't come out?"

We nod our heads.

"Well, what's done is done. You best all march down to see the nurse. I'm sure she'll have some solution to get it out. I'll come down in a few minutes to have a word with her."

Pulling out her pocket watch, she glances at it. "The dorms are off limits at the moment as we deal with a slight outbreak of lice from the petites."

Deirdra starts crying.

"Oh, good grief," Sister Jovita says. "There is no need to shed tears over this. It's not the first time it's happened here and it won't be the last. Now, hurry along, as I've got to strip the sheets," she sighs.

I suddenly remember Sister Francis's pictures in my pillow-case and the diary underneath my pillow. "I have to get something from my room."

"What could you possibly need?" Sister Jovita asks, her arms now folded across her chest.

Thinking like Fran, I say with a flushed face, "Um...supplies for my monthly cycle?"

"Very well. Off you go."

Relieved, I duck in and grab the diary. Now what? I can't just carry it out. I grab a bag from my armoire and shove it in.

"You haven't started your period yet, have you?" Fran asks as we go down the stairs.

"Eww no! I had to grab the diary and photos."

"I was going to say—"

"What are you two yakking about?" Deirdra says, suddenly stopping on the stairs. "It better not be about me."

The bird's nest on the top of her head is too much. "It's nothing about you," I start to say, but then I feel a smirk building and I look away.

"Oh, forget it. You two are so juvenile!" She whirls around and stomps off down the stairs.

"We better be nice to her—she might snitch on us for being in Sister Francis's room," I say, hugging the bag close to my chest.

"You've got a point. Won't be easy, but I'll try."

The smell of antiseptic hits me once we go through the infirmary doors.

Everything comes slamming back. *"Dotty doesn't have long to live...."*

I try to push the memories away as we walk down the long hallway towards the nurse's office, but some memories get burned into your brain and can't be erased.

Chapter 18

❖

"DEIRDRA IS NEVER GOING TO LET THIS ONE GO," FRAN says while we wait outside of the nurse's office.

I'm barely listening to her. How many times have I sat in this very spot waiting for Nurse to say it was okay for me to visit Dotty?

"Grace!"

"What?"

"I wonder what her 'Daddy' will think of her new hairdo."

"Oh! I forgot to tell you, she's not going on her trip."

"What?" Fran sits up.

"I found a telegram from her dad when I was looking for the shampoo. He said he was going to Sweden with some lady."

"Beatrice?"

"Yeah, that was it."

"But she told us—"

"I KNOW. She was lying."

Before we can say another word, Deirdra screams at the top of her lungs, "You can't! I won't let you!"

"What on earth is the screeching about?" Sister Jovita asks, marching up the hallway.

"Nurse is with Deirdra," I answer, now sitting on the edge of my seat.

"Deirdra's throwing a wobbler," Fran says.

Sister Jovita glares at Fran, then knocks on the door and slips into the room.

"Well, if anyone can throw a hissy fit, it's her!" Fran says, folding her arms. "God forbid anyone mess with her precious hair. I mean, look at us. We're not exactly beauties right now either." Fran shapes the top of her hair into a tall spike, then wipes the Vaseline from her fingers onto her pants.

I touch my hair, cringing at the thought of smothered lice in it.

A few minutes later, Nurse opens the door. "Girls, you may come back in."

Deirdra sits by the sink looking pale. Nurse has a concerned look on her face. "It's about your hair," she says. "It's the worst case of lice I've seen in a long time."

"But we were only with the petites for half an hour yesterday," Fran says.

"You've clearly had lice for longer than that," Nurse says, "and with the amount of Vaseline you've managed to massage into your hair, it's rather difficult to deal with. As you've discovered, it's very hard to get out! There appears to be only one solution."

Deirdra starts crying again.

"I'm afraid we have to shave your hair off."

Fran gasps.

Nurse says to Sister Jovita, as she's plugging in the electric razor, "I think it's best the girls sleep in the infirmary for the night. We don't want to alarm the rest of the students, as shaving may not be necessary for everyone."

"You mean I have to stay here? With them?" Deirdra says, lifting her head.

"What? You don't like our company?" Fran barks.

"Francine! That's enough," Sister Jovita says. "I think we all need to ask the Good Lord for a little guidance and patience to keep our tempers in check. Perhaps we should all take a deep breath before we carry on."

"Who wants to go first?" Nurse asks, not wasting any time.

No one offers, so she picks me. I flinch when the razor tugs on my hair. Clumps of hair land by my feet. The blood drains from my face when I see myself in the mirror. I don't recognize the girl staring back at me. I can't believe all my hair is gone. Just like that. When the buzzing finally stops after Nurse shaves all three of us, Fran is unusually quiet and Deirdra can't stop sniffling and blowing her nose.

"Before I go," Sister Jovita says after getting us settled in the infirmary, "I want to remind all of you that true beauty lies within."

"Humph!" Deirdra mumbles as she rolls over on the infirmary bed, causing the springs to squeak.

"God sees the inside, Deirdra. Your hair will grow back. It's not going to do you a speck of good to dwell on this. I know this has been difficult, but if you look, there's always a lesson in the hardship." Her keys clink together as she leaves the room.

Fran sits cross-legged on the bed across from me with her head in her hands.

"If you *look,* there's always a lesson in the hardship," Deirdra mimics. "You and your stupid ideas, Fran!" She flops back down and rolls over, placing the pillow over her head.

"Okay, so my plan didn't quite work out—I'm so daft!" Fran says.

"It's not your fault," I say, getting up from my bed and walking towards hers.

Fran rubs her freshly shaven head. "I can tell you one thing. I'm going to need a hat. My head is freezing!"

I touch mine. It actually hurts a bit and feels so strange, and yet I'm just relieved there aren't any bugs in my hair now.

Fran looks at me, smiles, and then rubs my head like a bowling ball. "You know, you don't look half bad."

"I think we all look disgusting," Deirdra barks from underneath her pillow. "I can't go on my trip looking like this! Thanks a lot, Grace! If only I hadn't been your dance partner!"

"You heard Nurse. You didn't catch this from me! Besides, I'm getting tired of your constant complaining. Your precious hair *will* grow back, like Sister Jovita said. Why don't you grow up?"

"Why don't *you* grow up—and realize you're just an orphan?!" Deirdra shoots back with her arms folded across her chest.

"Well, at least I don't *lie,* Deirdra."

"What are you talking about?"

"Don't play dumb, Deirdra. I know you're not going away with your dad. I read the telegram he sent. And to think you were trying to make *us* feel badly that you might not be able to go because of your stupid hair. I may not have any family, but I can tell you one thing, I'd rather be me than you any day!"

There. I've said it.

For the first time ever, Deirdra is speechless.

"Oh boy," Fran mutters under her breath as she stands up and walks over to the doorway to peek out. "You two are a ball."

I glance over at Deirdra. She's got her pillow over her head. I feel a pang of regret, followed by fear that she might tell on me for being in Sister Francis's room.

Just as I'm about to say something, Fran says, "Uh-oh, trouble on the way. Sister Francis is coming."

I zip back over to my bed and slip my hands underneath the pillow to make sure the diary is hidden. My heart pounds in my chest. What if she's already discovered that her pictures are missing?

She enters the infirmary with a tray of food and then stops in the middle of the room and stands there like she's seen a ghost when she notices our shaved heads. Her face goes pale and then she starts whispering to herself in French. I can't make out what she's saying, she's talking so quickly.

Fran and I glance at each other.

"Um...that smells good," Fran says, breaking the silence.

Sister Francis turns towards her voice, but seems to stare right through her.

"The food—it smells yummy," Fran repeats herself. "Is it for us?"

Sister Francis looks down at the tray she's holding. The glasses clink together as her hands start shaking violently.

Before I have time to grab the tray from her, she collapses to the floor and sobs uncontrollably.

Deirdra perches on the edge of her bed and Fran and I look at each other, not knowing what to do.

"Is everything all right in here?" Nurse asks, poking her head into the room.

"We didn't do anything," Fran whispers.

Deirdra joins Fran and me. I link arms with Fran as we watch Nurse try to calm Sister Francis down. For a second it reminds me of when Dotty would collapse on the ground in a puddle of tears, but that was sweet Dotty—not Sister Francis.

Chapter 19

✢

WHEN SISTER JOVITA RETURNS LATER ON, HER EYES look tired and worn out.

"Is Sister Francis okay?" Fran asks.

"She's resting comfortably. Dr. Graham is with her."

"Fran says she's gone barmy," Deirdra says.

"I did not—"

"That is quite enough," Sister Jovita says. "I'll not hear another word on this subject! I suggest you put your heads down, say your prayers, and get some sleep. You've all had quite a day." Before leaving, she adds, "I'll leave a torch on the table in case you need to use the toilet in the middle of the night." She places it on the little table by the door, then leaves.

The day's events are swirling around in my head. I keep hearing the sound of the electric razor buzzing in my ears and the look on Sister Francis's face just before she fell to the floor. "Fran, I can't sleep, can you?"

"Not blooming likely," she answers back. "My head is freezing, and I'm—"

"Would you guys stop yakking?!" Deirdra whines. "I'm totally knackered!"

Fran and I are quiet for a few minutes, but it isn't long before the silence is broken.

"Do you think the Red Nun is real?" Deirdra suddenly asks in a whimper.

"Afraid she might come and visit?" Fran says.

"I'm serious, Fran. Do you think maybe she had something to do with Sister Francis going barmy?"

It's weird to hear Deirdra sound so pathetic. She's usually so full of herself and comes across as though nothing upsets her.

"Who's the Red Nun?" I ask.

Fran sits up in her bed. "You really want to know?"

"Why did I bring it up?" Deirdra moans before covering her head with her pillow.

"So, the story around the Red Nun," Fran says, "is that she died a horrible death a gazillion years ago. I can't believe you haven't heard about it. Well, anyways. There's a legend that her foot got cut off and it's buried in a shoebox somewhere in the grounds. She's haunted the convent ever since." Fran pauses and then says, "Anytime something unexplained happens, the Red Nun gets blamed. That's why no one wants to sleep in here. Look, her photo is right over there by Deirdra's bed."

Sure enough, the moon lights up a picture of a woman's head and shoulders in a red veil and robe hanging on the wall. Deirdra muffles a squeal and whips off her blankets, and the next thing I know she's huddled on my bed, shaking like a two-year-old.

"Oh, you're such a nitwit, Deirdra," Fran says slipping out of her bed and grabbing the torch. Two seconds later, Fran joins us on my bed. "Move over, Deirdra."

We move around in my single bed until we're all huddled together like sardines.

"Hey, what's this?" Deirdra says, picking up the diary. Sister Francis's photos fall out when she opens it. The picture of her riding a bike in her nun outfit stare at us. "This is what you nicked from Sister Francis's chambrette, isn't it?"

Blood drains from my face and I feel a bit dizzy. Fran closes the curtain to my bed then shines the flashlight in Deirdra's face. "You can't say anything about this, and yes the photos are hers!"

"Why did you take them?" Deirdra asks.

"None of your business!" Fran says.

"I'll snitch on you if you don't tell me."

"Sister Francis took my photo album of my sister, and I was looking for it in her chambrette when I found these pictures," I hiss. "I just haven't put them back yet."

"And what about the diary? Do you know who it belongs to? And why are you reading it?"

Sighing, I say, "We found it in the library, shoved in one of the shelves. We're using it for Fran's history project. This person lived in the convent during the war. And no, we don't know who it belongs to."

"You can't say anything about this, Deirdra," Fran says, shining the light in her eyes again.

"I'm not daft," Deirdra says, shielding her eyes.

"Promise?" I say.

"Yes...yes! I promise." The excitement in her voice is annoying.

"We might as well read some more now that we're wide awake," I say. "Fran, can you hold the light?"

"Sure."

I turn past more damaged pages until I find another legible one and read it out loud.

February 4, 1945
Dear diary,

Time has a way of standing still when you wish for it to speed up. Today the bells rang for the first time from the belfry.

We haven't heard it for such a long time. It brought tears to my eyes, because while everyone is rejoicing that the allies have liberated Belgium, it can't bring back what I've lost. I fear Mother Superior is noticing that I'm more withdrawn into myself. If she only knew about the night the Nazi solider attacked me, she might understand, but I can't tell her. I fear she'd send me away, and I have nowhere to go. So far, I've been able to hide my growing stomach underneath my robe. Lately I've been having sharp pains in my stomach and I'm getting scared. I'm not sure I can do this—again.

Fran and I glance at each other and say at the same time, "she's pregnant?"

"Okay, you guys have to fill me in," Deirdra says. "What is she talking about?"

"Deirdra. We don't have time," Fran says.

"Let me see," Deirdra says, grabbing the diary.

"Don't be such a pain, Deirdra. Give it back!"

"What on earth is going on?" Nurse booms, scaring us.

I snatch the pictures and shove them with the diary underneath the pillow before she whips open the curtain.

"I had a nightmare," I say swallowing hard. The lies clog my throat.

"Don't make me regret opening up the infirmary to the three of you. Get into your own beds, and not another peep!"

In the middle of the night, I hear someone crying.

"Is that you, Deirdra?" I whisper.

She doesn't answer. "Deirdra?" I say again. I hear her roll over.

Sighing, I say, "I'm sorry I read your telegram."

Deirdra doesn't say anything. I roll over and hug my pillow. Dotty's voice whispers, *"Juth breathe. Ith okay,"* but it's not. Things are downright terrible.

I try to go back to sleep but can't. When I notice the torch, I decide to read some more of the diary. Fran is snoring, so I don't bother waking her. I sneak underneath my blankets and continue reading.

I finally had word via telegram that Mother and Father are alive, but Mother is not well. Mother Superior has arranged for me to have safe travel to visit for a fortnight.

I'm afraid to see Father. I hope he has forgiven me by now.

There are a few illegible pages, and then:

The village where my parents live is unrecognizable, with house after house burnt to the ground. Villagers are still removing the last remaining black-and-red Nazi flags that had been hanging everywhere. I never want to see another one as long as I live.

Mother was relieved to see me, but Father still had the hurt in his eyes, which quickly turned to anger when he noticed my growing stomach. He flew into a rage about how I have betrayed the family, church, and God a second time. I pleaded with him to help me, that it wasn't my fault, but Father said I was a disgrace to the church and an embarrassment to us all. He forbade me to have any more contact with them after my visit. Mother had pity on me and took me, in her frail state, the next day to a nearby guérisseuse mystique. She gave me something to drink which will help speed the baby along. I have no one to turn to. Not even God. The war has not just hardened my soul—it has taken it.

Chapter 20

✠

"I'VE GOT STUBBLE!" DEIRDRA SHOUTS FROM THE LOO.

"Oh, blimey. I can't take it," Fran says. "Is she ever going to stop?"

"At least you didn't hear her talking in her sleep," I grumble. "Between my own bad dreams and her mumbling, I feel like I've been awake all night."

"And to think we're probably stuck with her all day!" Fran complains.

"I can see you're all awake and alert," Sister Jovita says, walking in unannounced. She opens up the curtains. When she turns around, it looks like she hasn't slept either. "I trust you've said your morning prayers?"

"We just finished," Fran mumbles.

"Is Sister Francis okay?" I ask, changing the subject.

Worry creeps over Sister Jovita's face. "She's quite fragile at the moment, but it's nothing for you to worry about. She's being looked after. I'll be in charge of your dorm for the time being."

Fran and I exchange glances. I feel like doing a jumping-up-and-down Dotty dance, but when Deirdra returns from the loo, her mood evaporates any lightness I'm feeling. Her face is all blotchy from crying.

"Dear, you really must pull yourself together," Sister Jovita says. "Things could be far worse than losing your hair for a spell. You'll be happy to know that your father rang last night."

"Is he coming to get me?" Deirdra asks.

"No, dear."

Deirdra's face falls.

"He suggested that when the rest of the girls head home for half-term, a trip to the village store to buy a few treats might be in order. He also requested that you be able to take a friend with you. As you know, the trip to the village store is usually reserved for the seniors. This is a huge privilege. One I do not give out lightly. Fran will be going home, so perhaps you might consider inviting Grace? I'll make arrangements for Monday morning once you let me know."

Deirdra walks over to the window and looks out. The sunlight bounces off her bald head, showing stubble and some weird bumps at the back. Good thing she can't see them. Spinning around, she says, "I can't go looking like this!"

"I have a kerchief you may wear," Sister Jovita sighs. Her voice sounds sympathetic and impatient at the same time.

After a few moments, Deirdra mumbles, "I'll think about it."

"Those going home for half-term will be leaving at scattered intervals," Sister Jovita says, picking up a tissue that has fallen out of her robe pocket. "Thankfully, we managed to treat everyone for lice yesterday. I'll expect the three of you to get dressed for church. Fran, check with Kitty to find out what time your train is leaving."

Deirdra sniffs every two seconds.

"Do you think she might take me into town?" I ask Fran once we're out of earshot.

"I don't know, but let's hope so. You could check out the address from your file. You still have it, right?"

"Yeah, it's in my pocket."

The dorm feels lighter without Sister Francis standing guard at her little desk. Kitty stands in her place while Sister Jovita is busy. Unlike Sister Francis, who would glare at you when you'd enter the dorm, Kitty gives us a warm smile.

Deirdra dashes to her chambrette when the girls notice our bald heads and start laughing. I'm surprised that Deirdra's friends are among the ones pointing and laughing.

At her.

Maybe she'll get a taste of what it feels like to be made fun of. I hear Dotty say, *"Juth breathe. Ith okay,"* which makes me hold my head high as I walk by the open mouths and wide-eyed stares.

Fran, on the other hand, uses this opportunity to ham it up by bowing in the middle of the dorm, as if she's a court jester. "Take a good look, girls," she announces. "We're sporting the latest fashion. Coming soon to your nearest hair salon. You too can look as smashing as us. Just get yourself some friendly lice and—"

Everyone laughs.

"Come on, Fran," Kitty says. "Mass is in ten minutes."

While sitting in church during the endless prayers, where I usually tune everything out and daydream, I'm suddenly struck with a thunderbolt of panic when I realize I've left the diary and the photos under my pillow in the infirmary. Fran is two rows ahead of me, so I can't tell her. What am I going to do? If someone finds it before me, I'll be in so much trouble.

Luckily for me, there is no proclamation this Sunday. As soon as Fran and I are able to talk, I tell her about the diary.

"We'll just tell Nurse we've forgotten something. Come on."

When we enter the infirmary, it's empty. I scramble over to my bed and reach underneath the pillow. Nothing. I check under the bed.

Empty.

No diary.

No pictures.

I feel like throwing up. I drop to the floor on all fours and look underneath the bed.

Nothing but dust bunnies.

"Okay, this isn't good," Fran says, glancing around the infirmary. "Right. Let's go outside where we can talk and figure out what we're going to do."

The grounds are unusually quiet; most students are packing for their trip home. This used to be the time of year that Dotty and I loved the best, when we could roam freely without the threat of the girls giving us a hard time, but I'm not feeling like anything good is going to come of this break.

"What am I going to do?" I blurt out. "I might as well just run away. Once they find out I stole Sister Francis's pictures and the diary from the library, I'm done for. Mother Superior told me there were going to be no second chances."

"Well, if you run anywhere, it will be to my place in London," Fran says. "If you go down, I go down." Fran holds out her pinky finger. "Promise."

"Oh, Fran. Why weren't we friends long ago?" And then I remember Dotty. She'd be so happy that Fran and I were friends. "You know, Dotty always liked you."

"Proper girl, that Dotty," Fran says, linking arms with me. "Now, we have to figure out something."

We end up walking through the paths that lead us to the back of the grounds. "You know," Fran says, "while everyone is busy packing and the nuns are dealing with all the dorms, we could sneak into the village and get some *frites*. You never get away, and if Deirdra doesn't invite you with her, this is your only chance. Come on. We can easily climb the wall. No one will ever know. It will be fun. Besides, we could check out the address from your file."

I glance at the stone wall, easily twelve feet high. "Do you think we really could?"

"If someone can land on the moon, I think we can scale the wall, but we better run back to the dorm to get some clothes to change into. We'll be a dead giveaway in our uniforms."

"Let's do it."

Back at the dorm, we try to act very casual, but inside I'm a mixture of panic and excitement. There's only a handful of girls in the dorm. Deirdra is one of them. She's sitting on her bed with her knees tucked against her chest. She looks sickly with her hair gone.

It's funny how I thought she was so pretty before. Now she just looks plain. Not that Fran and I look any better.

I rummage through my armoire and grab some plain clothing and a hat to wear. Within a few minutes, Fran and I are ready. Just as we're about to leave, I remember the address I scribbled down in Mother Superior's office. A surge of excitement rushes over me as I say a quick prayer that the mysterious person who sends me money knows how to find my mother.

"Where are you going?" Deirdra says, suddenly appearing with her arms folded across her chest.

"Outside."

"Yeah, but where? I've been watching you pack. You two are up to something."

"Blimey, Deirdra. Can't you leave well enough alone?"

"I can easily tell about the photos and—"

"Fine," Fran says, pulling her into the chambrette and explaining.

It's like a switch flips in Deirdra. "I'm in. Let me get some stuff."

And just like that, we're stuck with Deirdra. Again.

Chapter 21

⬧

CLIMBING THE WALL TURNS OUT TO BE TRICKIER THAN we thought, especially with Deirdra's constant complaining, but for some reason she seems as determined as us to do it.

Luckily, we find a tree near the wall. We shimmy up to the first limb and then use it to help us get on top of the wall.

Fran is the first one to make it. "I swear we're lucky," she says, sitting on top. "Someone placed a bunch of hay bales from the field right below us. We can easily jump down onto one of them."

"Well, stop your nattering and do it," Deirdra barks. "I'm barely hanging onto this branch as it is."

One by one we cling from the tree branch, fling ourselves onto the wall, and land on the hay with a thump.

"I feel like a convict escaping prison, don't you?" Fran says, glancing back at the wall we just climbed.

"I can't believe we're doing this," I say.

"Well, I'd say we better get a move on if we're going to have time to enjoy our frites before we head back," Deirdra says. "It's not like we have all day."

Fran and I glance at each other. Since when is Deirdra ever helpful? Something doesn't feel right about her being with us, but I push my feelings away because she's right. We don't have much time.

"So, do you think we'll really be able to figure out who's sending me money?" I ask Fran as we dodge hay bales in the field.

"Fingers crossed," Fran says.

We walk in silence, each of us with our own thoughts, until we reach a wooden fence that is super easy to climb over. The village is one street over. I glance back towards the convent. It looks smaller the farther we get away from it.

"So, where do we have to go?" Deirdra asks.

I unfold the piece of paper I tucked safely in my pocket. "1359 Rue du Vaartdijk, Tildonk," I say, looking up at street signs. Narrow stone houses and shops line the village's main street.

We bolt down the street, checking signs as we go, but we can't find Rue du Vaartdijk. Fran stops at the corner where a man is selling frites from a portable stand. She asks for directions in French, but the man starts speaking in Flemish, so we can't make out what he's saying. While Fran orders, I say, "Maybe we shouldn't have come."

"Let's go to the village candy store," Deirdra suggests after we get the frites. "Someone there might know where it is."

Fran and I glance at each other and then at the same time say, "Sure."

The bells on the store's door clang and bang as it swings open. The lady behind the counter has grey hair and chin hairs that dangle like a Billy goat's. She looks like she's a hundred years old, the way she's bent over. Deirdra picks up a *Seventeen Magazine* and flips through it while Fran gets directions.

"It's just one street over," Fran says, turning around to us.

"I'm going to stay here and read while you guys check it out," Deirdra says.

"Suit yourself," Fran says, nudging me towards the door. "We'll be right back."

I glance back towards the store before heading across the street. Deirdra watches from the window. I get a funny feeling in the pit of my stomach. "I don't like that we're splitting up," I say once we've crossed the street. "What if Deirdra runs back to the convent and snitches on us? It would be so like her."

"Forget about Deirdra. She's probably found an article about boys or something."

"I guess you're right," I say, following Fran around the corner.

"I think we've found it," Fran says, pointing to a sign that says, "Tildonk Bakery and Garden Shop."

My heart sinks to the bottom of my feet. Why would someone from there be sending me money? "It must be the wrong address."

"Let's go check it out anyway," Fran says. "They're probably not open on Sundays, but we can at least peek through the windows."

Just as we're crossing the street, a truck pulls up in front of the shop. The driver gets out and starts unloading supplies. We cross the road quickly. A car zooms just behind us and honks. We see the door to the bakery open as we reach the other side. I stop dead in my tracks. Monsieur Castadot and his son, Ethan, greet the delivery man to help with the supplies.

"Look who it is," I gasp. "We're going to be in so much trouble."

Before we duck out of sight, Monsieur Castadot notices me. "Ma petite. What are you doing in the village?"

"Oh, hello. It's a long story," I say. "Please don't tell the Sisters we were here."

Fran butts in. "We need help with something." Fran pushes me towards Monsieur Castadot. "Show him the address, Grace."

I hand it to him.

"She's apparently been receiving money from this address for years, although she just found out," Fran carries on. "Grace is trying to figure out why she's getting it and if maybe whoever's sending it might know how to reach her family."

Monsieur Castadot clears his throat and is about to say something when someone yelling in Flemish causes us to turn around.

"Crikey! I don't believe it," says Fran.

Deirdra is sprawled out on the cobblestone road and a man on a bicycle is yelling at her. The fruit and vegetables that had been in his basket are strewn all over the road, causing cars to stop suddenly. Deirdra scrambles to her feet and darts off.

"What is she doing?"

"I don't know," Fran says. "But we better go find out!"

Several cars cut off our run and we have to wait to cross.

"Perhaps you should stay here," Monsieur Castadot shouts while we wait for the cars to pass.

"We can't. Please don't say anything," I yell back as we run across the street.

By the time we get to the other side, Deirdra is gone. "Which way did she go?" I say.

"Maybe that way?" Fran points and runs down a side street. I follow right behind her.

"It's no use," she says at the end of the street. "She's gone." She bends over to catch her breath.

"She can't just disappear into thin air," I say, feeling the panic in my voice.

"Where *is* she?!"

And then a tram rumbles past us, with Deirdra sitting in the window seat. Just like that, the tram disappears around the corner and out of sight.

"What is she doing?" Fran's voice sounds just as panicked as mine. "This is so like her, to pull a stunt like this. We should never have taken her." For the first time, Fran actually seems scared, making me nervous too. "I think she's running away," she says.

A loud horn startles me. I turn around. Monsieur Castadot pulls over in his truck and rolls down his window. "Did you find the girl?"

"No," I answer, almost bursting into tears. "She jumped on a tram. Where is she going?!'"

"Hop in, we'll go look for her."

We squeeze into the front seat and keep our eyes peeled for Deirdra as we bounce along the cobblestone road. My stomach feels like I've swallowed rocks as Monsieur Castadot swerves through the side streets.

Deirdra's nowhere. The tram is long gone.

"Where could she have gone?" I ask, barely getting the words out. I lean my head against the window. "This is all my fault." Tears sting my eyes. "Why did she run away?"

"How should I know?" Fran barks. "It wasn't part of the plan."

Monsieur Castadot turns the truck around when we hit construction and get stuck with a man holding a stop sign. "We better head back to the convent. This situation is bigger than the three of us."

We sit in complete silence on the ride back. At the sight of the black iron gates of the school, dread washes over me and my stomach twists around like a giant pretzel. Maybe Mother Superior is right. I do need to learn to trust myself and to know what is right and wrong. I should never have climbed the wall and run off into the village. What was I thinking?

Why did I listen to Fran?

Chapter 22

❖

FRAN AND I ARE WHISKED AWAY TO SEPARATE ROOMS before we can say anything to each other. "Kneel down, face the wall, and don't move until you're summoned," one of the nuns orders.

Everything is going so horribly wrong.

I listen to a bustle of activity outside in the hallway. Loud voices, one of them sounding like Monsieur Castadot. Why is he upset? Why is he being dragged into all of this? I can't stay on my knees. I rush to the window and see a white nun-mobile roaring out through the gates, leaving a puff of black smoke behind it. Then it hits me how serious this is.

I pace back and forth. Why did Deirdra run away? What if they can't find her? And what am I going to tell Mother Superior? I wish I could talk with Fran so that we could at least say the same thing. She's so good at coming up with excuses. I glance back out the window, hoping to see Deirdra walk through the front gates, but instead my mind wanders back to the diary entries, to when the Nazi attacked the girl. I wonder if this is the same window she looked out. I wonder what happened to her after she went home. I slump to the floor, realizing the diary is most likely in Mother Superior's hands now and I'll never find out what happened to her. And then reality hits me. It doesn't really matter what happened to that girl.

That was then. This is now.

What really matters is what is going to happen to me. I hug myself and rock back and forth. Dotty's voice whispers in my mind, *"Juth breathe. Ith okay."*

The wall clock quietly ticks away. When I realize they're not coming for me anytime soon, I curl into a little ball and fall asleep on the floor.

✣

Mother Superior is busy jotting something down on her pad of paper when I'm led into her office several hours later. When she glances up, I curtsey and say, "I'm really sorry for everything—"

She raises her hand for me to stop.

"But I have to explain. It's all my fault—"

"I've heard plenty today from Fran and Deirdra," she says, interrupting me.

"You found Deirdra?"

"By the grace of God, yes."

My huge sigh of relief is quickly replaced with fear. What did Deirdra say? Did she tell about me being in Sister Francis's room and taking her pictures?

"I'll take the strap right now," I say, trembling. "You told me no second chances, and—"

"Grace! For heaven's sake," Mother Superior says sternly. "Sit down. I've had enough drama today."

I immediately follow her orders and sit down.

"No one is giving you the strap." Taking a deep breath, she softens her voice, adding, "but I gather from Fran that you received the strap from Sister Francis after the dreadful incident with the makeup. Is this true?"

I nod, glancing at the scars on my hands.

"Bless you, child. That should never have happened. And to think you never said a word." Mother Superior stands up and walks over to the window. "I also understand that it was Deirdra who put you up to defacing the statue in the garden."

Tears well up as I nod my head again. I can't believe Deirdra owned up to that!

Sighing she says, "I feel we have failed you, Grace."

Failed me? What is she talking about? I'm the one who has failed.

A knock on the door startles me. Mother Superior walks over to open it. She talks in hushed voices with one of the Sisters, then turns to me. "An urgent matter has come up, Grace—we'll have to finish this discussion later."

Something is not right. She didn't ask me about what happened in the village. She wouldn't let me speak at all. I dart upstairs to the dorm to find Fran, but no one's there. Deirdra's chambrette is completely empty. I run over to Fran's. Her bed is stripped. Her armoire doors are open and all her clothing is gone. I turn around and check my own armoire. All my clothes are exactly where I left them. I flop down on my bed and shake uncontrollably at the thought of my only friend being gone. I let out a loud wailing cry when I see Sister Jovita enter the dorm.

"What did you do with Fran and Deirdra?"

"They're gone, Grace. Sent home."

"What do you mean, sent home?" I sob.

"Grace, we can't have students being untrustworthy. The fact that Fran stole Sister Francis's keys, went into her room, and took her belongings is inexcusable! She was sent home with the last group of girls on the train a few minutes ago."

I feel vomit rise in my throat. "Did Deirdra tell you that?"

"No, Deirdra had other things to share, but that wasn't one of them. Fran gave herself up."

"But—but—I was the one who went into Sister Francis's room. I took the pictures, and the keys were for me."

"Good Lord in Heaven!" Sister Jovita says. "Why on earth—

"Because." I can barely breathe. "Sister Francis took the photo album that you gave me of Dotty. She said horrible things to me about her—said I was an embarrassment just like her. I didn't mean to keep the pictures and the diary we found in the library."

Sister Jovita's face softens. She gently sweeps hair away from my eyes, and in the most calming way, says, "You're not an embarrassment and neither was Dotty."

I collapse into her arms. Everything I've been holding in for so long rushes out like a stream during a rainstorm.

⁜

Sister Jovita and I march through the corridors to find Mother Superior. We pass the dance hall.

I lean over the banister and think of the diary entries, trying to imagine soldiers filling that space.

"Grace!" Sister Jovita says. "Stop lollygagging."

"Sorry," I say. I'm brought back to the only thing that matters—making sure Mother Superior knows Fran didn't do anything wrong.

Sister Jovita makes me sit outside while she talks to Mother Superior. I strain to hear what they're saying, but all I hear are muffled voices.

She told me there would be no second chances. What will she do when she finds out I stole the pictures? Will she send me away like she did Fran?

Where would I even go?

The sleeve of my shirt is wet from wiping my eyes, which keep filling up no matter how hard I try to stop them. Just as I am about to turn into a big puddle, Sister Jovita opens the door. "Mother Superior wants to talk to you now."

I enter the room and curtsey but avoid glancing at Mother Superior. Sister Jovita sits in the chair next to the window. I sit directly opposite Mother Superior. She removes her glasses and takes a deep breath.

The little diary sits on the desk, looming as though it were a hundred times bigger. I close my eyes and brace myself.

"Juth breathe. Ith okay."

Chapter 23

⟐

"THINGS HAVE BECOME RATHER COMPLICATED, AND
I'm not quite sure where to begin," Mother Superior says. She
picks up the diary and fans the pages. The beginning pages of the
diary are no longer stuck together. How did she get them unstuck
without ripping? "Some things in life are hard to understand
ourselves, let alone explain."

Pause.

"Exactly where did you find this diary?"

I squirm. "In the library, stuffed behind some books on one
of the shelves. I only meant to borrow it. Fran was doing research
on the convent and we thought it would help."

Mother Superior clasps her hands together and glances
towards the window. "Well, this diary has answered a lot of questions we've had over the years."

"You mean about the war?" I ask.

"No, Grace. I wish it were that simple—"

Loud voices in the hallway interrupt her.

"Would you mind investigating?" Mother Superior asks
Sister Jovita.

Before Sister Jovita reaches the door, it swings open and in
barges Monsieur Castadot.

Mother Superior immediately rises. "I beg your pardon. What on earth do you think you're doing? Did we not conclude our discussion earlier?"

"She needs to know the truth!" he bellows. "Look at her, for God's sake—she's a child, with her whole life ahead of her. It's time she knows. I beg you to do the right thing!"

What is he talking about? I glance back and forth between the two of them, both looking like bulls ready to fight.

"Monsieur Castadot, please, not now," Sister Jovita says, gently placing her hand on his arm. "I promise we'll discuss things with Grace, but just this moment is not the time." She tries to shoo him out, but he refuses to leave.

"Tell the child. I'm not leaving until you do!"

I face Sister Jovita. "What is he talking about?"

Sister Jovita closes the door.

Mother Superior gestures for Monsieur Castadot to sit down. "Very well, as you wish," she says with a heavy sigh.

I don't know what's going on. I glance at Sister Jovita with a puzzled look.

"It's about your family history," Mother Superior says.

"I don't understand. I thought I didn't have any." My voice cracks. "Sister Jovita told me that."

Sister Jovita is about to say something, but Mother Superior cuts her off.

"Well, it's somewhat delicate, and we've only just put the puzzle pieces together," she says, then stands up, reaches into a file behind her, and pulls out a newspaper article.

She places it on the desk and slides it towards me. "This is where your history begins."

I reach for it and stare at the photo of a nun holding a baby in her arms. The caption reads, "Baby infant found on the steps of the convent."

"Is that me?"

"No, dear." Her eyes soften. "That was Dotty."

"I don't understand."

Mother Superior carries on. "When I took up my post after the late Mother Superior, I was not told anything other than a baby was left on our steps. For some reason, she felt it was best if I didn't know all the details. I never understood quite why, until now." Mother Superior shakes her head and says, "Never in a million years did I suspect that the baby left on the convent steps belonged to one of our own Sisters."

"What are you telling me?"

"Well, from what we can gather, Dotty was left on the steps of the convent by one of our Sisters. During the war, the Nazis ordered widespread killing of the sick and disabled. Dotty would have been included. It wasn't just the Jewish people that they hated."

Mother Superior shifts in her seat and looks like she's struggling for words. "You see, the diary you've been reading belongs to...Sister Francis."

My mind races as I think about the diary entries. It can't be true. And then I remember reading the entry where she went home because her mother was sick and her father said she was a disgrace. It must have been because she was pregnant with the baby. "But—but that means she is my mother as well. She's too old!" My entire body starts shaking. "I don't believe you!" I yell. "I was left on the steps as a baby! That's what you've always told me!" I glare at Sister Jovita. "You said. Remember?!"

Sister Jovita gently takes the newspaper article from me and places her hands on my shoulders. "I'm so sorry," she murmurs.

"Actually, Grace, it's a little more complicated than that," Mother Superior continues. She shifts in her seat again and takes a deep breath. "There is no easy way to say this, but Dotty...." She clears her throat. "Dotty was actually your mother. Not your sister."

My brain explodes like fireworks. Each thought goes in a completely different direction. None of this is making sense. I knew Dotty was older than me, but never did I *ever* think she might be my mother. It doesn't make any sense. How could she be?

Mother Superior carries on. "At the time, it was felt that it would be easier if you thought she was your sister, considering the struggles she had. It was not an easy time after you were born. You must understand that we made this decision with the best of intentions. Dotty never knew who her birth mother was."

And there it was.

The truth laid out before me in black and white, just like the newspaper article.

"Grace," Sister Jovita says gently. "Just breathe. It's going to be okay."

Her words slam into me. I can't catch my breath.

"We're still in shock too," Sister Jovita says gently. "We would never have placed you in Sister Francis's dorm if we knew—"

"I—I need to go...." I bolt out of the chair and rush towards the door.

"Grace," Sister Jovita pleads. "There's more you need to know—"

"I don't want to know anything more!" I sob, before glaring at Monsieur Castadot. "How could this possibly make me feel better?" Tears sting my eyes.

"Ma petite—I'm so sorry." He reaches for my hand, but I pull away.

Out of the corner of my eye, I notice the diary sitting on the edge of the desk. Without hesitating, I lunge towards it.

Mother Superior grabs my hand. "Are you sure you want to carry through with this?"

A sudden burst of rage rips through me as I snatch the diary and wriggle it out of her hold. "Yes!" I scream.

I hear Sister Jovita say, "Let her go."

I run down the hallway without looking back. Everything is a blur as I dodge past students in the hallway on my way outside. Some laugh when they see my shaved head. Others look worried, but I don't care what they think.

I just need some fresh air. I need to breathe.

Chapter 24

✦

BY THE TIME I END UP AT THE GROTTO WHERE DOTTY and I used to hide, my chest is burning. If I don't stop to rest, my lungs will rip into tiny pieces. But I can't stop. I don't want anyone to find me. It won't be long before they come looking for me. I decide to stop just for a minute, bent over behind the grotto, and try to catch my breath. Why is this happening? Fran was supposed to help me with my family tree. My mother was supposed to come back for me.

All my thoughts are crowding each other out, competing for my attention. One momentarily beats the others: No wonder we didn't get put in the sister dorm. We were never sisters!

I shake my head. That doesn't make sense. How could she have a baby? She was more like a kid than an adult. And if she was my mother, who was my dad?

Quickly, another thought shoves that one out of the way. Sister Francis is my grandmother. I start shaking controllably. Hugging my stomach, I rock back and forth. Fran gone, Dotty gone, no one I can trust. I am more alone than ever before. I don't know what to do. I hear Dotty's voice in my head: *"Juth breathe. Ith okay."*

"It's not OKAY!" I scream. The diary I've been clutching falls to the ground, and the photos of Sister Francis fall out.

"Do you hear me, Dotty?!!! Everything is *not* okay. Look at these! They're of your *mother*!" I pick them up and wave them in the air as if Dotty is standing right in front of me. "Your horrible, evil mother, who left you on the steps of the convent and then pretended she didn't know you. She was *awful* to you, and to me. She is the worst person in the whole world. I hate her," I sob. "And to think I was stupid enough to think I had a mother. That she was going to somehow come and find us. That it was all just a horrible mistake that she left us at the convent. How STUPID!" I yell.

I rip up one of the photos into small pieces, then wipe the snot from my nose. "Everyone lied to us, Dotty—even Sister Jovita!" I'm about to rip another photo when I stop and stare at the photo of Sister Francis roller skating in her long grey dress and habit. Was this before she got pregnant? Or was it afterwards? Something makes me pick up the diary. I turn to where I left off. Maybe Mother Superior has it wrong and this diary doesn't belong to Sister Francis. I mean, how does she know? The person has never mentioned their name anywhere. How can she be sure?

February 18, 1945
Dear diary,

I feel so alone. No one understands me or what I'm going through. Father told me that I was being punished for my sins by giving birth to a mongoloid child. He instructed me to hand the baby over to the nuns. He had me so terrified about the baby's condition that I did the only thing I could think of, or at least I tried, but I was so weak by the time we reached the convent that I collapsed just outside of the gates. From what Mother Superior told me, I almost bled to death. I also don't remember much except that when I came around, I was in the infirmary and the baby was not with me. I remember immediately thinking she had died, and part of me was relieved, because then Father might forgive me and I could return home. I never wanted to be a nun. I was so weak and confused that everything is a blur, but my talk with Mother Superior remains crystal clear in my mind. She was the one who found me outside the gates. She was the one who placed the baby on the steps of the convent to make it look like another unwanted pregnancy had occurred. And she was the one who made me promise to never speak of it for the rest of my life. I signed papers then and there that I would have nothing to do with the baby. In return, they would look after her. In a blink of an eye, my body and soul were ripped away from me yet again.

I reread the entry, then flip to other entries, trying to understand, trying to make sense of everything. It can't be her. It just can't!

When I was stronger, Mother Superior let me know that while Father has publicly disowned the baby and myself, he will continue to make payments to the convent to cover the costs. Mother Superior let me know that raising a child with the baby's limitations will require a huge sacrifice from the Sisters and that in exchange I was not permitted to have any involvement in raising her. She also reminded me that I had chosen a life of sacrifice when I took the white veil; a life where one is detached from family, things, and the past.

I'm not permitted to speak aloud for a full year as part of my continued training and inner discipline. I'm forbidden to have any contact with the baby and I must be obedient in all things until death.

I feel so badly for this girl. There's no way it can be written by horrible, cruel Sister Francis—this girl is so sad and scared. Mother Superior has to be wrong. It doesn't make any sense. I frantically flip through the diary, going back to the beginning so I can prove that they're all wrong. I find an entry I don't remember. This must have been one of the pages stuck together before.

June 5, 1942
Dear diary,

Father dropped me off this morning. After meeting with Mother Superior, he handed her an envelope, thanked her for helping him, then abruptly left me standing in the front foyer of the convent without even saying goodbye. I never wanted to come here, but because of the war and the embarrassment I have caused him, he said there was no alternative.

"A fifteen-year-old is not in a position to have a baby."

But I want our baby. I don't want to give it up for adoption. Hugo is kind and thoughtful and he loves me, but the war has changed everything. He left a fortnight ago to fight for our country. When the baby moves, I feel like Hugo is right here with me. He reassured me that he'll come for me when the war is over. Mother Superior seems to have pity on me and she has helped me get settled in.

She had *two* pregnancies? One from this Hugo person when she was fifteen, and then one from the Nazi?

"*Juth breathe,*" I hear Dotty say.

"I can't, Dotty!" This is too confusing. With no mention of Sister Francis's name, I don't allow myself to believe them. "It's NOT her!" I yell.

I continue reading.

January 18, 1943

Dear diary,

My baby died a month ago. I'm numb. I have no way of reaching Hugo. He promised he'd write, but I have yet to receive any word from him. I'm working long hours in the laundry until my contract is up. Father signed a three-year work placement in exchange for housing the baby and myself. What if I can't find Hugo when my time is up? Where will I go? I have no one.

"Who *are* you??" I yell. And then I read:

Before I signed the vows, Mother Superior reminded me of our secret and that I am never to speak of it and that I have to hold it as my highest form of obedience and penance. After signing my vows, Mother Superior cut my long hair with a pair of kitchen scissors. After my hair was cut, Mother Superior took the clippers and shaved my head. She gave me my new name before placing the habit of humility on my head. From now on, I shall be known as Sister Francis.

And there it is. I close the book and weep.

Chapter 25

✦

I'M NOT SURE HOW LONG I SAT BEHIND THE GROTTO, and I can't really remember how I ended up back in the infirmary, but somehow that's where I am, and have been for a few days.

"I'm taking a vow of silence," I mumble from underneath my blankets when Sister Jovita comes to see me. "I'm not talking to anyone!"

Sister Jovita sits down on the bed. "Grace, you can't just hide away." She sounds like she's at the end of her rope.

"You lied to me," I mumble.

She takes a long deep breath. "Grace, for the hundredth time, from the bottom of my heart, I'm truly sorry." She sits quietly for a few minutes before saying, "We did what we thought was in your best interest. I wish we could turn back the clock and do it differently, but we can't." Sighing, she says, "You might like to know, though, that I found your photo album."

I don't say anything.

"Very well. I'll leave it for you. Perhaps when I return in an hour you'll be dressed." She doesn't wait for me to respond, instead saying in a gentle voice, "We all have to learn how to handle disappointments, Grace. Life isn't always easy, but finding grace to accept what is, helps one move forward."

Once her footsteps fade, I peek out from underneath my blankets to make sure she's really gone, then shove the blankets off and reach for the photo album. I stare at a photo of Dotty with her head tilted back, mouth wide open, laughing. Who knows at what? To Dotty, the reason behind the laughter never really mattered. In one photo, Dotty has her baby doll tucked underneath her arm with just its head peeking out. She must be at least sixteen or seventeen years old. I flip backward to see if she had her doll with her when she was a little girl, but she doesn't in any of the photos. In all the photos where she's older, she has the baby doll, by its feet or by one arm. I never really thought much of it when she was alive. I just figured it helped her while I was in school to have someone to talk to, or something to hold. Dotty would read to her baby doll, with the book upside down most times, and sing to it endlessly, to the point where I'd tell her to stop because it was getting on my nerves.

Did they give the baby to her after she had me? I have flashes of memory, of Dotty getting out of bed in the middle of the night, wandering around the corridors until she'd end up at the infirmary, inconsolable. Was she looking for her baby? For me? Did she know that her doll wasn't real? Maybe that's why she always said, "Be back thoon," at bedtime. She knew she'd left her baby somewhere, but didn't know where.

If only she'd known she hadn't. If only she'd known that she was with her baby all along. And then it hits me. How would I have felt? Would I have been okay knowing she was my mother? Or would I have been so embarrassed that I would have been horrible to her? If I had known the truth, things probably would have been different. Maybe Sister Jovita was right.

She did what she thought was the best for me, and for Dotty.

⁜

I'm ready for Sister Jovita when she returns an hour later. She looks relieved when she sees me dressed, but she doesn't say anything except, "It's beautiful out. Let's get some fresh air."

We walk along the paths for quite a while without talking. The brisk air fills my lungs and clears my brain. I finally blurt out, "I don't want to grow up to be angry like Sister Francis. I won't be like her when I'm older, will I?"

Sister Jovita puts her arm around me. "No, dear." She points to a bench nearby. "Let's sit." She adjusts her robe and wraps her shawl snugly around her.

"It's just...she was so mean to Dotty and me," I say, fiddling with the sleeve of my sweater, twisting it inside and out. "Why was she like that?"

Sister Jovita sits quietly for a few seconds before saying, "The war did horrible things to people, and some never recovered. It was a different time in the convent as well. Had we known Sister Francis's past, I'd like to think we would have made sure she had proper counselling. It appears that what she lived through had a very damaging effect on her. And to think she was only sixteen when she wrote this. At least now she's being tended to and will hopefully get some much-needed help."

"Is that why she collapsed in the infirmary?"

"I don't really know, but I suspect that seeing the three of you with your heads shaved must have brought back everything she's been trying to forget."

I think about her diary. *After signing my vows, Mother Superior cut my long hair with a pair of kitchen scissors. After my hair was cut, Mother Superior took the clippers and shaved my head.* I think about her first baby dying, giving up her second baby—and how her family rejected her—and then I remember that she never told her Mother Superior about being attacked by the Nazi, and that her boyfriend never came back to get her. But what sticks out is that she never, ever wanted to become a nun.

And here she was, stuck looking after children that reminded her of what she couldn't have.

"What I've discovered," Sister Jovita says, jarring me out of my thoughts, "is that if we push troubling events in our life aside, they eventually bubble up and show themselves in the most unusual ways. She's had a lot of losses in her life, and she has suppressed her feelings for far too long. I can only think that perhaps things caught up with her, but I can't say for sure."

I glance around the gardens. Most of the leaves have fallen from the trees, leaving everything lonely and bare. I think about the diary entries from after Dotty was born.

"It's just—am I...."

"What is it, dear?"

"Well, um...how am I supposed to repay the convent for looking after Dotty and me? Because I read in Sister Francis's diary that she had to repay the Sisters for looking after Dotty... um...and I really don't want to be a nun."

Sister Jovita laughs from the bottom of her belly. She puts her arm around me. "No one expects you to become a nun or to repay us anything. Things were very different back then. Often in those days, when an unwanted pregnancy happened, a family would send the young woman to a convent to have her baby in private. The child was then adopted out to a family who couldn't have their own. In return, the young woman worked for several years in the convent to repay her room and board. I'm saddened to say that in some cases those girls were sorely mistreated, but things are not like that now. Our only hope is that you will go on to do good things in your life, and that you'll practise forgiveness and kindness along the way." She squeezes my hand. "I believe learning how to weave in and around our difficulties with grace is our life's lesson." Then she points towards the graveyard. "He's been here every day, hoping to see you."

I glance to where she's pointing and notice Monsieur Castadot walking along the path.

"Why?"

"I'll leave that for him to explain." She pats my leg as he gets closer. "Please listen with an open heart."

Sister Jovita stands to greet him, then leaves us alone.

I study his face. Worry and fear have taken hold in the furrow of his brow, but kindness and love radiate from his eyes. "May I sit down?"

I nod.

"Please forgive me, ma petite. I didn't mean for things to go the way they did the other day. That was not what I wanted Mother Superior to share with you. In fact, I was unaware of Sister Francis's past."

"What did you want them to tell me, then?"

"Well," he begins after a moment, "I made a promise years ago to the Sisters. One that I deeply regret, but at the time it seemed best for everyone involved."

He takes a deep breath. "You see, Ethan used to spend his days with me here in the gardens. He and Dotty were fast friends. The Sisters and I thought it was all very innocent until the day Sister Francis found them together behind the grotto, and we quickly discovered there was more to their friendship. When Dotty became pregnant, we realized their relationship was more than any of us could cope with."

He pauses.

"To make matters worse, my wife was dying, so we did the only thing we could." He clears his throat. "Ethan was sent away, and he never knew about you. We felt that was for the best. I regret doing that now." He takes a deep breath and carries on. "I know that the money I sent every month for you will never make up for all of this."

I turn towards Monsieur Castadot. His eyes are filled with sadness.

"The money came from you?" My voice sounds like a mouse's squeak.

"I wanted to make sure you had presents on your birthday and clothing when you needed it. I know it wasn't much. And I don't expect you to understand, but I do hope with time you'll be able to make a place for Ethan and me in your heart. I'm so sorry, Grace."

I glance away, uncomfortable at seeing how badly he's hurting. I'm not sure what to say. I stare straight ahead at the paths weaving in and around the gardens, thinking about my own path to knowing Ethan is my dad.

"How is that possible? I mean...how come I don't have Down syndrome?"

Monsieur Castadot sighs. "Ethan was born healthy, but when he was a day old, he was fast asleep in his crib. It had been a busy day at the hospital and the poor lad choked on his own saliva. The nurses didn't notice until he was blue in the face. He lost oxygen for one minute too long, causing damage to his brain. Otherwise he would have led a completely different life." He takes a deep breath. "But then you wouldn't have been born. So in a way, it was a blessing."

I try to take everything in. My head feels woozy. I remember singing to Dotty after she had a nightmare. I remember saying goodbye, missing her, then being relieved I didn't have to worry about her anymore.

"What are you thinking, ma petite?" His voice is gentle and soothing.

"It's just...I'm not sure I can do the same things for Ethan that I had to do for Dotty." I feel bad when I hear the words out loud.

He puts his arm around me. "Dotty was very lucky to have you, but you've had enough burdens in your life. I would never want to add to that." His voice cracks. "I want you to enjoy being a child. I think once you get to know Ethan, you'll be pleasantly surprised at how easygoing he is. You just need to be his friend. Nothing more. Besides, I'm fit as a fiddle, I'm not going anywhere." He pulls me close. "I'll spend the rest of my days making it up to you—that is, if you'll let me."

I blink back tears.

Chapter 26

❖

"BLIMEY!" FRAN YELLS THROUGH THE PHONE. "ARE you all right?"

"It hasn't really sunk in yet," I say, twisting the phone cord around.

"So, let me get this straight," Fran carries on. "She had a boyfriend named Hugo and got pregnant when she was fifteen, so her dad sent her to the convent to have her baby? And the baby died and then she became a nun when she never heard back from her boyfriend?" Fran's listing everything off so fast she sounds like she's an announcer at a horse race. "You're dead serious?"

"Uh-huh."

"And then she got pregnant with Dotty from that horrible Nazi? And the Mother Superior—the one before ours—left her baby on the steps so no one would know it was hers? You're really not fibbing?"

"Nope."

"Do you think her boyfriend died in the war?"

"I guess. Maybe."

"You must be gobsmacked. I sure am." Fran continues blabbering on like she's afraid of any dead air. "You know...I bet the nuns withheld letters from Hugo. It would be like them to do that. I bet he wrote to her. That's kinda sad."

"Why would they have done that?"

"Oh, Grace. I keep forgetting you don't get letters each week. All our mail is read by the nuns before we get it. Even the letters we send home get read before they're mailed out. That's why it's such a joke that we have to write home each week; we can't really say anything bad or it will get crossed out. I bet they destroyed all her mail."

Fran doesn't realize she's carrying on the conversation all by herself. I'm quietly realizing we're not just talking about horrible old Sister Francis—we're talking about Dotty's mother, my *grandmother*. My thoughts continue to be jumbled and confused. Am I suddenly supposed to forgive her after all she's done and said, just because we're related? And yet I can't stop thinking about what she wrote in her diary. She wasn't always mean, and she did have really horrible things happen to her. Maybe Sister Jovita is right about the war making people unable to live with peace in their hearts anymore. Sister Jovita says it's okay for me to have mixed-up thoughts about it. I think she secretly does too.

"Um—Grace...you still there?"

"Yeah, I'm here. I was just thinking about everything."

"I'm sorry," Fran says. "I'm going on as if I'm talking about a show on the telly."

"It's okay. It *is* like a TV show—I just happen to be stuck in it! Imagine finding out Sister Francis is your grandmother? I keep having nightmares about it."

"Ick! But that's fab news about Monsieur Castadot! They were beastly not to tell you sooner about him! I'd fancy him for a grandfather any day. And what about Ethan, you okay with that?"

"Yeah, I guess. I don't really know him. It's sort of like having Dotty here. At least now I know why she always said, 'Be back soon' at bedtime."

"Why?" Fran asks.

"Ethan says the same thing whenever he says goodbye." I close my eyes and smile, thinking about the day we told Ethan.

"Ethan, there is something we need to tell you," Monsieur Castadot said, putting his arm around me. "Remember Dotty?"

"My Dotty in heaven?"

"Yes, your Dotty in heaven," Monsieur Castadot said gently. "Well, Grace is Dotty's daughter. She has been brought to us for good."

"For all the days?"

"Yes, for all the days, Ethan."

He patted my head. "Little Princess Grace," he repeated over and over. "For all the days."

"Earth to Grace"—Fran jars me back—"I never told you about Deirdra!"

I can't believe I haven't thought about her. I've been so absorbed in my own life that Deirdra has not once filled space in my brain. "Oh, yeah. Do you know what happened?"

"Yeah, I guess she wanted to get kicked out, so she ran away. They found her at the end of the tram line. She ran out of money and had nowhere to go. She wanted to get sent home, but not to her dad's. She went home to her mum's. She and I sat together on the train home. I've never seen her so brutally honest about how she was feeling. It was like the old Deirdra was sitting across from me. Have to say, I did feel badly for her when she told me about her stepmum hitting her, and that her dad just ignores it."

"Wow. Didn't you say she'd run away before?"

"Oh, that's right. I'd forgotten about that, crikey! We could write a book about all the goings on," Fran says, giggling into the phone.

"I wish you were here," I say.

"Half-term will be over before you know it. Thanks to you, I've been given the green light to return, but mum has threatened me to within an inch of my life that there are to be no more shenanigans."

"Mother Superior said the same thing to me." I glance at the wall clock. "We'd better get off. Sister Jovita said I could only talk for a few minutes." Just before I hang up, I remember something. "I forgot to tell you that Monsieur Castadot is going to help me with my family tree for History. I'll be able to do it after all."

"That's brill."

"Hey, Fran?"

"Yeah?"

"I miss you."

"Me too."

Chapter 27

⬦

EVERYTHING FEELS DIFFERENT NOW, LIKE A BUTTON missing on your shirt or your shoe missing its laces, but I'm getting used to having bits and pieces of my life missing here and there. I still miss Dotty, but that's to be expected. Or, that's at least that's what my counsellor tells me.

Monsieur Castadot, Papa, insisted that I see a counsellor he knows in the village, someone not related to the convent, to talk about my feelings. Sister Jovita and Mother Superior thought it was a really good idea as well. Papa is paying for it, and says I can go for as long as I need to. I really like her, and it does feel good talking about stuff, even though I was a little nervous at first.

Before my next counselling session, which is tomorrow, I'm supposed to write down everything I'm thinking. The counsellor said to pretend that I'm taking a shovel into my brain and scooping out all my thoughts onto paper—no matter what they are. And, when I'm finished, I'm not to read one single sentence. Instead, I'm to rip it up into small pieces. She said it will help me get rid of the thoughts of Sister Francis that keep haunting me at night, as they're buried deep inside of me. I may have to do it several times until the thoughts get fewer and fewer.

The sky looks like it's going to dump buckets of rain any minute. I stare at the empty page, but before I start writing, I slip off my bed and close the curtains to my chambrette.

I start writing about one thing and then I find something completely different pours out of me, but the counsellor told me to expect this, so I don't worry about it. Once I start, I can't seem to stop.

When I can't think of anything else to write, I put my pen down. I'm about to read what I've written, but then remember I promised the counsellor I wouldn't. She told me, "If you reread it, you'll start churning the thoughts around like a gerbil running in its wheel."

I don't want that to happen, so I immediately rip it up into tiny pieces. Staring at what then looks like a really tricky jigsaw puzzle spread across my bed, I feel tears well up.

The counsellor warned me that this might happen too, and she said it was normal and not to worry about it.

Then I remember ripping up the photo of Sister Francis when she was younger. I never did figure out if it was taken before or after she gave birth to Dotty. I'd like to think it was before—when she was happier.

A loud crack of thunder rattles the windows, followed by buckets and buckets of rain pouring out of the sky. Dotty hated thunder more than anything. I'd have to hug her and the baby doll while I sang to them until the storm had passed, each and every time.

Where is her doll? Then I remember Sister Jovita giving me a box with some of Dotty's things in it. I hadn't wanted to root through it before, but now I need to.

I scoop up the paper and dump it into the garbage, then search for the box underneath my bed. Lying gently on the top of Dotty's favourite pink sweater, the one I made Sister Jovita keep, is her baby doll. I lift her out and stare at her little pink face and her sparkly blue eyes that close when you lie her down. I hug her and breathe in the last bit of Dotty.

And then it hits me. I know what I need to do.

It takes a bit of convincing before Sister Jovita lets me visit Sister Francis. She has to get permission from the doctor first.

"Are you sure you're up for this?" she asks. "You're doing so much better. I'm fearful of you going backwards."

"As long as you come with me, I think I'll be okay. I don't want to be scared of her anymore."

It's been two months since I've seen Sister Francis, but I've thought of her ever since. When we reach the cloisters—the part of the convent where "the nuns who are off their rockers live," according to Fran—I feel a little nervous. What if she yells at me? What if I chicken out and bolt out of here like Dotty would do? And then I hear Dotty's voice.

"Juth breathe. Ith okay."

And I remember she can't hurt me anymore. Never again.

Sister Jovita enters first and walks over to where Sister Francis sits in a chair in front of the window. She puts her hand gently on her shoulder and talks quietly to her. I try to make out what Sister Jovita is saying, but can't. I'm not sure I can move. My legs feel like they're glued to the floor with a ton of bricks sitting on my chest.

After a few seconds that feel more like hours, Sister Jovita waves for me to enter. I force my feet to move forward. It feels like giant weights are attached to them. Maybe I shouldn't have come. What was I thinking?

Sister Francis continues to stare ahead as if we're not even in the room. I was warned that she was heavily medicated.

"Grace has something she'd like to give to you," Sister Jovita says gently.

My hands shake as I hold out Dotty's baby doll, all worn and tattered, but deeply loved. It takes a few moments for her to respond, but she eventually reaches out and takes it. She clutches it tightly to her chest, then starts rocking back and forth. She doesn't say anything or even look at me. I'm secretly relieved.

Sister Jovita nods that it's time to go. She murmurs something to Sister Francis before we leave. It sounds like, "It's going to be okay. You have your baby now."

Just as I'm about to walk away, Sister Francis lifts her head. Her eyes are filled with tears. I panic when she reaches for my arm, but Sister Jovita puts her hand on my shoulder and whispers, "Just breathe. It's okay."

It takes Sister Francis a few minutes to get her words out, but in a quiet whisper she says, "Merci."

I let out a huge sigh of relief when we close the door behind us. Sister Jovita puts her arm around me and says, "Are you okay?"

I swallow, unable to use my words, then nod to let her know I'll be fine. When the last door clicks shut behind us, I decide to leave the past where it belongs.

Chapter 28

⬥

ETHAN PUSHES ME BACK UP THE HILL IN A wheelbarrow after one of our visits to Dotty's grave. With winter snow now settled across the ground, we probably won't visit again until the spring. I listen to him chatting away about nothing and everything. Every now and then he breaks out into laughter, which makes me join him.

I hope Dotty can hear us.

"Come on, you two," Papa says. His smile matches the twinkle in his eyes. "We've got to help Grace put the finishing touches on her History project."

Ethan makes a loud grunting noise as he picks up his step. I glance up towards the part of the convent where Sister Francis now lives. Sometimes I think I see her staring out the window holding the baby doll, but maybe it's just my imagination.

As we walk by the frozen frog pond at the front of the convent, a cold breeze bites the back of my neck and makes me shudder.

"Can we have hot cocoa when we get to home?" Ethan asks.

"That sounds like a splendid idea," Papa says. "Perfect for Christmastime."

Back at his house, Papa lights a fire while Ethan and I get the hot cocoa ready. Ethan talks to himself as he reaches for things.

"Cocoa, check. Milk, check. Hot water on, check." He repeats himself until he's satisfied. Then he looks at everything and says, "We're missing something."

I don't want to make him feel funny, as he's so proud to be getting everything all organized, so I pretend to be puzzled for a few minutes before I say, "Maybe mugs?"

He points his finger at me and smiles before saying, "My Princess Grace is smart." He then opens the cupboard and whispers to himself, "Mugs, check."

I smile.

❖

Mother Superior and Papa decided I should stay at the convent for now, until things get sorted out. I'm okay with it, because Fran is here and Dotty is everywhere I turn, especially now that Sister Jovita is minding our dorm. Besides, I visit Ethan and Papa every weekend and sometimes Fran comes with me.

Today's the first day back after the Christmas holidays, the day we present our History project. My stomach flutters as I wait my turn. In a brief flash, I think about the first time I sat in this room, staring at the empty page of my family tree, and how everything has changed. All my life I thought my mother had abandoned Dotty and me, and she was with me all along. Dotty loved me more than anything. This I know for sure. I'd like to think that maybe somehow she brought Ethan and Papa into my life right when I needed them the most. I glance around the classroom. Out of the corner of my eye, I notice Papa slip quietly in. Sister Jovita said he might come to see my presentation.

I stand up, walk to the front, turn, and face the class. I glance over at Papa. He gently nods his head as if to say, "You can do it."

My fingers tremble as I sort out my paper. And then I hear Dotty's voice. *"Juth breath. Ith okay."* And I realize I really do believe things will be okay. I take a deep breath and say, "My mother's first name was Dorothy, but we called her Dotty." Pause. "It means gift of God...."

⚜

March 16, 1975
Dear diary,

I've been thinking a lot lately about when I went to see Sister Francis—probably because I had a counselling session a couple of days ago. I keep wondering if she feels badly about all the horrible things she's said and done, but I'll never know. At least I feel good about what I did.

The counsellor said that I was really brave and should feel really proud of myself for giving her Dotty's baby doll.

So I guess, in a way, I did what Dotty would have done. She never stayed mad at people. When she noticed someone was sad, she'd try to cheer them up. How many times did she shove that same baby doll into my arms to make me feel better?

I'm so glad Papa gave me this diary. The counsellor is right—it does make me feel better writing down my thoughts. I keep thinking about the little dessert shop in the village where Papa and I went after my first session. I can still taste the lemon sherbet in a scooped-out frozen lemon. The sherbet was stuffed to the rim. It was the best dessert I've ever had. Papa said we'll make a habit out of it.

Okay, I better say goodbye now, because Fran and I are going roller skating, even though it's freezing cold out. I know we're probably bonkers, but that's okay. Thanks for listening to me blabber on.

Be back soon.

Acknowledgements

THIS HAS BY FAR BEEN THE MOST CHALLENGING STORY I've written to date. I can't tell you how many ways I've attempted to tell this story—and for that, I have to thank my writing group: Lisa Harrington, Graham Bullock, Joanne Yhard, and Jennifer Thorne, who over the years have listened patiently to every single version.

Thanks to my editors, Emily MacKinnon, Whitney Moran, and Penelope Jackson. Their belief in this story and keen editorial insights helped me dig deeper, and for that I will be forever grateful. Not to mention they are the best group of ladies to work with. Dream team for sure!

Thanks also to Karen Barrett Pranschke, who I've never met in person. She took the time to email back and forth when I had questions about the convent. Her willingness to jot down the tiniest of details and to offer up her insights and suggestions was so helpful. I couldn't have done it without her.

To the TOGS (Tildonk Old Girls Society) who have visited the school over the years and have posted photos on our Facebook page, THANK YOU. Stumbling on our site at a time when I was doing research on the school was divinely orchestrated.

Everyone needs someone in their corner to cheer them along, and thankfully my family takes this job very seriously. My parents are my biggest cheerleaders, but my husband and my cousin Alison Rodgriguez come in at a close second—for this, I am truly grateful.

GRACE GREER

DAPHNE GREER GRADUATED FROM Mount St. Vincent University with a Bachelor of Child Study. She is the author of *Maxed Out*, a 2013 nominee for best quick read by the American Library Association, the sequel, *Camped Out*, a 2018–19 Hackmatack nominee, and *Jacob's Landing*, which was nominated for the 2016 Silver Birch Award and 2016–17 Hackmatack Award. She lives in Newport Landing, Nova Scotia, with her husband and four daughters. Visit her at daphnegreer.com.